"Who pays for all this?"

Ellis's face had gone hard. "Your lawyer friend?"

"No," Sorrel said sharply. But remembering the contempt she had seen in his eyes for women who preyed on older men, she would not in any case have told him about kindly old Mr. Ollerenshaw. "In fact," she continued, and wanting him out of there, she brushed past him to hold the door wide, "the man who pays for my—life-style—is no one you know."

He went on his way, despising her, thinking she was some man's kept woman. How much more would he despise her if he knew where the money for her expensive apartment and all its trappings had come from!

Books by Jessica Steele

HARLEQUIN PRESENTS

HARLEQUIN ROMANCE

These books may be available at your local bookseller.

Don't miss any of our special offers. Write to us at the following address for information on our newest releases.

Harlequin Reader Service
P.O. Box 52040, Phoenix, AZ 85072-2040
Canadian address: P.O. Box 2800, Postal Station A,
5170 Yonge St,. Willowdale, Ont.   M2N 6J3

JESSICA STEELE

facade

Harlequin Books

TORONTO • NEW YORK • LONDON
AMSTERDAM • PARIS • SYDNEY • HAMBURG
STOCKHOLM • ATHENS • TOKYO • MILAN

Harlequin Presents first edition March 1985
ISBN 0-373-10767-6

Original hardcover edition published in 1984
by Mills & Boon Limited

CHAPTER ONE

A POISED, sophisticated woman stared back from her bedroom mirror. Sorrel was well pleased with her reflection; it had been hard won.

Downstairs Roderick Drury had announced his arrival. She let him wait—sophisticated women, she had learned, did not rush to any man's bidding.

She checked the perfection of her make-up, her hands smoothing the elegant skirt to the well cut suit she had on. But a warmth, that had no part in her new image, was to trip her up as she thought of the man who had made it possible for her to have the expensive apartment that went with her recently acquired expensive clothes.

Dear old Mr Ollerenshaw, she thought, recalling that she had been the only one to fight back tears at his funeral. She, apparently, the old one to regret the passing of the worn old ex-scrap metal merchant who had been far more wealthy than she had ever realised.

Warmth went from her as that thought was followed by the memory of the fuss his daughter had kicked up when she had learned the contents of his will. That Cynthia Armitage had inherited the greater part of his fortune had been neither here nor there when Cynthia had gone for her. Indeed, so livid had her employer been that she had screeched a whole volley of spiteful invective at her before she had pitched Sorrel out on her ear.

Had it not been for Mr Ollerenshaw's specific wish

that she 'live a little', his messsage that she had more than earned a good time, and the gentle but not to be denied blackmail of, 'I shall not rest peacefully in my grave should you refuse my gift,' then Sorrel would happily have told Cynthia that she did not want a penny of the amount he had left her.

Not that the money would have then gone to Cynthia anyway. For, as clever in his will as he had been in the investments that had made him his fortune, Albert Ollerenshaw had stated that if Sorrel turned down what to her was a massive gift, then the money was not to go to Cynthia, but, of all things, into research into the mating habits of the common fieldmouse.

Only the fact that it might prove costly to have her dead father certified as of unsound mind had prevented Cynthia from going along that course, Sorrel knew.

But he hadn't been potty. Neglected by his daughter, certainly, for all they lived in the same house, but his mind had been sharp to the end. She should know; she had been with him when he had died while Cynthia was out somewhere living it up.

Sorrel reached for her overnight case on the bed, determined then that she was not going to give another thought to Cynthia Armitage. But her breath caught, as with the thought that Cynthia Armitage need not think that she had the sole rights to sacking her on the spot, she was reminded that it had been done before. Eight years ago, to be precise—though of course that didn't hurt any more.

Locking her flat behind her, Sorrel took the lift in the smart block down to the ground floor. Her sophisticated exterior allowed a smile to her mouth but not to her eyes as, not apologising for keeping Roderick Drury waiting, she greeted him coolly:

'On time as usual.'

'And as usual, you look stunning,' returned the twenty-nine-year-old lawyer, who would like to have rushed their relationship, but wisely, having once been put very firmly in his place, now appeared content to let things go along at the pace Sorrel would allow.

Seated beside him as he negotiated the car out of London and headed it towards the Kent countryside, Sorrel had not missed the way his eyes had lit up when he had seen her. And other thoughts she did not want; thoughts that maybe Rod had more than a passing interest in her gave her some moments' irritation.

She knew all about this smart set she had joined six months ago. Years of living in the same house with Cynthia and her weak, pathetic husband Leslie had shown her that, while they might have affairs by the dozen, hearts were not hurt on either side. But while she had not the smallest intention of having an affair with Rod Drury, or any other man for that matter, if Rod looked at her with the same eager light in his eyes many more times, then without doubt, she would soon be telling him that she wasn't going to see him any more.

'Your parents do know that . . .' She halted. Rod turning his fair head to look at her made her aware that her sophisticated exterior was in danger of slipping. But, having started, she summoned up a cool smile and made herself continue. 'Your parents are aware that there's no special significance in my spending a night in your home, aren't they?'

Rod gave her a warm smile, and turned his attention back to his driving. 'Relax, Sorrel,' he told her easily. 'I'm always taking girls home.'

Her fears calmed, Sorrel turned her head to stare out

of the window, not sure she wanted him to know that she had been a little uptight back there for a moment.

By the time he had driven the car round a wide drive and had pulled up in front of a large house fronted by perfectly manicured lawns, she had herself in hand again, her manner detached as she stood with Rod waiting to be introduced to the two people who had come out into the June sunshine to greet them.

Moira and Neville Drury were nice people, she discovered, with a passion for horses. With a promise to show her the stables, Sorrel refraining from telling them that she did not ride, the four of them went indoors.

'You'll want to freshen up after your journey, I expect,' suggested Moira as they went along the hall. 'I'll get one of the maids to show you your room.'

'Thank you,' Sorrel replied pleasantly, and promising to join them for tea shortly, she went with the maid, aware that had she let the more natural Sorrel Maitland come through, then possibly Moira Drury would have shown her to her room personally.

But she did not want warmer contact with anyone. She had learned the hard way that if one was to survive, one had to keep one's warmer feelings hidden. Years ago she had been a warm impulsive person, in love with life, sunny-natured, in love with . . .

She turned her attention to unpacking the few things she had brought with her, wondering why she should suddenly think of *him*. He'd been out of her life for years now!

It didn't hurt any longer, she repeated firmly. And anyway, if years of seeing the superficial way Cynthia and Leslie Armitage had gone on while she had looked after their two children—not to mention the whole hive of drones who drifted in and out—wasn't enough to

teach her the fickleness of love, then her own
unrequited love when she had been sure her love had
been returned, added to what she had seen, had surely
taught her a thing or two.

She still hated to face the way she had thrown herself
at the man she had thought meant marriage when,
loving him, she had been prepared to do anything he
asked of her. Though she no longer blushed at the
memory, devils were at her heels as she remembered
how at seventeen her offer of her virginity had been
turned down. She'd made very sure no man had ever
got that close to her again.

'I hope I haven't kept you waiting,' she apologised, a
slight thawing in her manner as she entered the drawing
room. That thawing was due, she knew, to her trying to
eject thoughts that even now, eight years on, would still
occasionally return to haunt her.

Talk over the tea-cups was the superficial sort which
Sorrel could cope with quite easily. Her nanny duties
had often included standing in for a short while when
Cynthia Armitage, who was never on time for anything,
carried on getting ready upstairs.

As she listened to Rod's father telling him about
some house locally which had been on the market and
had recently been purchased by a business associate of
his, Sorrel's thoughts slid away from their conversation.
Her mind flitted back to Cynthia's father, and how it
had been only on account of old Mr Ollerenshaw that
she had stayed so long in that job. For with nobody
seeming to care whether he lived or died, how could she
leave even though she often wanted to?

She had been determined to leave the last time Leslie
Armitage had made another of his furtive passes at her.
But with Albert Ollerenshaw so shaky on his feet

towards the end, she had taken one look at the frail old man and had seen that if she wasn't there to pick him up and get him to bed the next time he fell down, then nobody else would bother.

Her thoughts drifted on to how, when she had come back from taking her two charges, the precocious Arabella and more lovable younger brother Benjamin out for a walk one day, she had returned to find the house full of noisy people, with the old man cold and unable to get up from the upstairs landing where he had fallen an hour before. When she had been able to make herself heard, neither Cynthia nor Leslie had been in the least troubled with what she had told them; it had been left to her to call a doctor. And left to her had been the nursing of him, Cynthia looking scandalised at the thought of spending good money on a nursing home or having a nurse in when Sorrel looked to be quite capable of taking care of her two offspring and her father. 'Live a little,' old Mr Ollerenshaw had said in his will . . .

Sorrel wiped the gentle smile off her face as her thoughts left Albert Ollerenshaw and she came back to her surroundings to hear that the new neighbour, apparently, was coming to dinner that night. Sorrel was pleased about that—it made it less as though she was someone special whom Rod had brought down to meet his folks.

'Would you like to see the stables?' The question, with an apologetic look to his mother who had made the original offer, had come from Rod.

'Very much,' replied Sorrel, unhurriedly getting to her feet.

Rod, she was soon seeing, had inherited his parents' love of horses. And she found herself warming to him more than she had done when, leaving her side, he went over to his favourite grey, and, forgetful that she was there, began crooning baby talk. His smile when he turned and saw her watching was more than a shade selfconscious.

'I never thought to tell you to bring your riding things,' he apologised to cover his embarrassment. 'Though I'm sure we can fix you up with some . . .'

'I don't ride,' Sorrel replied, honest with him suddenly where recently she had rather taken to giving evasive answers.

She waited for his appalled look, and warmed to him some more when he grinned, and said, 'I'm sorry. We horse-lovers rather take it for granted that everybody rides, don't we?' She smiled, and that light she didn't want appeared in his eyes again. 'I'd love to teach you if you'd care . . .' he began.

'No, thanks,' she said a touch sharply, and turned away.

In her room, she was pensive as she dressed ready for dinner. Her dress was an elegant full-length rose crêpe creation, sleeveless and with a square neck, but for the first time she was feeling no pleasure in having something lovely to wear.

It had been a mistake to come on this visit, she thought. Rod had been hurt by the change in her manner; and his hurt had showed. And the trouble was, she could not try and put it right by being warmer to him at dinner, because that would make him think that she was more interested in him than she was.

Thank goodness there would be other people at dinner. With the new neighbour there, and most likely his wife, Rod's parents were less likely to notice that their son was feeling bruised that his guest was not all over him.

Dinner was at eight, but in 'living a little'; in trying out the life she had only witnessed from an employee's standpoint, where Sorrel might keep an escort waiting for her, the roots of her strict upbringing were too deeply laid for her to keep a whole household waiting should she be late in going down to dinner.

At a quarter to eight, her thick light brown hair with its natural streaks of light gold done up in a classical knot, Sorrel left her room.

With calm and confidence she opened the drawing room door. A tall slim man with his back to her was in conversation with Rod and his parents when she went in. She saw the man make some kind of movement at Rod's welcoming, 'Sorrel!' and guessed he had politely turned to be introduced. But as Rod came towards her so her attention was distracted from the man she thought must be the new neighbour, for, temporarily blocking her view of the fellow dinner guest, Rod was standing in front of her.

'How beautiful you are,' was his greeting, to make her feel a mixture of being glad that he was over his hurt, and irritation that the eager light was there in his eyes again. But although she did not like it when he took hold of her hand, the next second Sorrel was never more glad to have something to hold on to. For quite without warning, as he remembered his manners, so he smiled, 'Come and meet Ellis Galbraith.'

With a roaring in her ears, Sorrel gripped tightly on to the hand that held hers. All thought of Rod Drury went from her head then—and every other thought. Just that name Ellis Galbraith gave her a violent need to hare back up to her room. Desperately then did she need to have some time in which to compose herself.

But Sorrel was to find that she had no time in which

to get herself together. For Rod had moved to the side of her and was taking her up to the man who had moved on Rod's welcoming cry of 'Sorrel!'

That Ellis Galbraith had received something of a surprise too was obvious from the look that seemed to say he could hardly believe his eyes that the sophisticated female facing him bore no resemblance to the white-faced seventeen-year-old, her hair flowing down her back, who had stood crushed before him eight years ago.

It was thanks to her knowing she looked good in her fashionable dress, thanks to all she had seen and heard in the past eight years, that Sorrel was able to get through the next five minutes. She thanked whoever else there was to thank, too, that no one could see beyond her outer covering to the quivering mess she was inside. Even her guardian angel was pulling out all the stops, she thought, for her voice was well modulated, and just this side of cool as Sorrel extended her hand to the terrific-looking man whom the last eight years appeared to have left no other mark than the few strands of silver in his night-dark hair, and a line or two on a face she would know anywhere.

'Rod has just said he'll introduce us,' she smiled, 'but there's no need, is there?' And while her senses took another battering as a firm hand came out and he shook hands with her, 'How are you these days?' she asked with another cool smile.

'You know each other?' Rod broke in before Ellis Galbraith had done anything but look steadily into her unsmiling green eyes. 'Everybody's heard of Ellis, I know,' Rod was going on, 'but I didn't know you knew him.'

The last thing Sorrel wanted was that any of them

should know a thing of what had gone on between her
and Ellis. She still bore the scars that she had once
worked for him, had once fallen heart and soul in love
with him, and for her pains, had once been instantly
dismissed by him.

'We used to live near each other in Wiltshire at one
time, didn't we?' she said, her smile still cool, her legs
weak as she waited for his reply.

'Many moons ago.' His voice was the same as she
remembered, deep, rich, as now he was rich, though he
hadn't always been as wealthy as the papers reported he
was today. But his eyes were still on her, his hand was
still holding hers, and when she was sure he didn't give
a damn who knew that she had in those early days of
him getting started been his Girl Friday, he was not
letting anyone listening know what a fool she had made
of herself over him. 'You're as lovely as ever you were,
Sorrel,' he said smoothly, his eyes flicking down to her
left hand, and back sharply to her face. 'What's
happened to you since the last time we met?'

That he could refer to that scene that had all but
finished her off without so much as batting an eyelid
gave Sorrel's stiffening the kick it needed.

'Oh, this and that,' she said airily. Graciously then
she retrieved her hand, presenting him with her profile
as she turned to refuse Rod's offer of a sherry.
Courteously she went over to have a word with her
hosts.

Somehow she got through dinner that evening.
Inwardly stunned, when she would by far have
preferred to stay quiet and let everyone else do the
talking, something in her pushed her not to let Ellis
Galbraith have the smallest inkling of how seeing him
again so unexpectedly had rocked her.

Never having thought she would be grateful to Cynthia Armitage for anything, memory stood her in good stead of the brittle chat that had gone on at her dinner parties when she had been roped in occasionally rather than have the table arrangements ruined when at the last minute someone failed to turn up.

More than once she was aware of Ellis's eyes on her as she joined in on any subject under discussion. It was almost as if he could not believe the tremendous change that had taken place in her—not only in appearance—from those days when it seldom had troubled her what she wore, to the not-a-hair-out-of-place, fashionable woman she had turned into.

'You live locally, Sorrel?' he asked her at one point when Rod's laughter had died away at some return she had made, and the subject matter swiftly faded from her mind at Ellis's abrupt question.

'I've always loved the country . . .' she said, and paused, smiling to Moira and Neville Drury as she only just managed to bite back the 'as you know' that so very nearly escaped her. 'But,' she added, a smile on her mouth as she turned back to him, his dark good looks so familiar to her yet absent for so long, 'London is where it all happens, isn't it?' she bounced back tritely.

'You live in London?'

His sudden interest, when for eight years he hadn't cared whether she was alive or dead, annoyed her. But she nodded, and found another insincere smile. 'And I love it,' she said, then smartly turned her attention to Moira Drury. 'Do you manage to get up to town very often?' she asked.

To Sorrel's great relief, the evening turning out to be more wearing than it had any right to be, in her opinion, as dinner drew to a close she heard Rod's father say there was a small business matter he and Ellis had to discuss, and charmingly he asked would they excuse them for half an hour.

Take a couple of hours, Sorrel wanted to say, but she smiled on as they moved to the drawing room with Moira chiding them not to be too long. 'I know what it is when a couple of redundant engineers get talking,' she joked.

'Redundant?' asked Sorrel, the moment the two men had departed.

'Ellis, like Neville, has had to leave the drawing board behind,' Moira explained. 'Nowadays, I believe, they both spend their working hours in the administration of their companies.'

It crossed Sorrel's mind to wonder how, with a head that had always been brimful of new ideas, Ellis had taken to being desk-bound. Although being desk-bound did not stop one from being inventive, she supposed.

'What would you like to drink, Sorrel?'

She looked up to find that Rod had come to stand near, but she shook her head. She wanted nothing to drink, rather did she want to be by herself.

'Nothing, thanks,' she smiled. 'Actually, all this country air has made me sleepy. I was wondering,' she added, turning to Moira, 'if you would think me rude if I didn't stay down too long?'

'Not at all,' Moira replied. 'As a matter of fact,' she confided, a warmth coming through that had not been there initially, 'since I like to have the horses exercised early, I rarely stay up late myself.'

That Rod looked disappointed that he would not have her sole company after his parents had retired had little effect on Sorrel. She liked him, as she was growing to like his parents, but that was all.

Though since she was his guest too, she stayed long enough to ask him if he had felt no inclination to join his father's firm.

'A sore point,' he admitted. 'Though I think Dad's got over it now.' And with a smile to his mother, 'It wouldn't have worked you know. I've no aptitude for the business.' And with a grin at Sorrel, 'I couldn't even put my bike chain on when it came off when I was a kid!'

Sorrel laughed lightly, and heard Moira telling her son that his father was keeping a place open for him in his legal department if he wanted it. But her interest was more in listening for sounds that would tell her that Ellis and Neville had finished their business.

They had been absent twenty-five minutes when Sorrel, after a small delicate yawn, latching on to the lead Moira had given that the two men could well not appear again until gone midnight, offered her excuses to them, and went to her room.

But, as in her heart she had known would happen, no sooner had she closed her door than she was travelling back to the time when, just seventeen, she had presented herself at the workshop-cum-office of Ellis Galbraith, and had instantly fallen in love with him. Day and night, then, she had thought and dreamed of nothing but him.

Ellis already had a worldly air about him in those days, a confidence that said he knew where he was going. He had qualified as an engineer, but where money had been tight when he had left university, he had had a whole wealth of inventive ideas that used to keep him working well into the night.

He had been twenty-eight when, totally frustrated at being unable to get any of the major firms interested in his inventions, he had scraped together every penny he could lay his hands on, going up to his neck in debt to his bank, to set up his own firm.

Within months he had been bogged down with paper work that interfered with the real work he should be doing. Already working over-long hours as he was, it was then that he had advertised for a Girl Friday, and she had gone to work for him.

And being in love with him, Sorrel had not minded what hours she put in either. For they had worked well together, she snatching at every crumb, hugging to her the moments when he would suddenly notice the time and say, 'Little Sorrel, I don't deserve you.' He would get out his beaten up old car then and insist on taking her home.

Oh, how she had loved those lifts home! They would talk all the way of the twelve-mile journey from the small town of Kinglingham to the tiny village of Salford Foley where she lived with her parents, and she would go up to bed and lie awake for hours, just thinking about him.

She had been strictly brought up, but her parents had met Ellis, and her father, a man who believed hard work was good for the soul, approved and applauded Ellis's industry and what he was trying to do. If Sorrel was often late home, then since she was working hard too, that was all right by him.

She had been working for Ellis for six months when the first breakthrough had come. Ellis had got a buyer for a small batch of his products. Vividly did she recall that day. It marked the day when she ceased to be just a pretty pair of ever-willing hands, to being a blossoming young woman with an eagerness to share with Ellis everything he could teach her.

Later she was to realise that he had hardly realised what he was doing when in his triumph after putting down the phone from that call that had given him his start, he had grabbed hold of her and had given her a rib-crushing hug in his exultation.

But her face had been near to his, and she was never afterwards sure whether he had kissed her, or if she had kissed him. But in any event, their lips had met, and she had clung to him, with no sign of backing away when he had raised his head and looked at her. What was in her eyes she had no way of knowing, but his quiet comment of, 'You're only a baby, Sorrel,' had seen her refusing to look away from his as she'd countered, 'For an inventor, you want your eyes testing!'

He had pushed her a little away from him, his eyes flicking to her burgeoning breasts to bring crimson colour to her cheeks, she recalled. But she had kept her hands on his shoulders, and as her blush had faded, so Ellis had kissed her again.

After that he had taken her out a few times, and she had begun to think of herself as his steady girl-friend. He would always kiss her when he took her home, either after a date or when he dropped her home when she had worked late. But that she had read far more in his off the cuff remarks than he had intended, only later, was she to crash back to earth and see how blind her love had made her.

Only later was she able to see that his, 'When I've enough black in that permanently red account at the bank, I'm going to do something about you, young Sorrel,' had not meant that when that day came he was going to ask her to marry him.

Painfully obvious later, she had come to see that all he had meant by that remark was that when funds permitted, Ellis intended to give her a whacking rise to make up for the small amount which was all he could afford by way of her salary each month.

But then all she had seen in his remark was what she wanted to see. Only she couldn't wait. She was seventeen, in love, and impatient to be Mrs Ellis Galbraith.

Remembering the confidence that had been hers at seventeen, the confidence that Ellis must love her, Sorrel winced again at the pain of it. For things had come to a head when he returned to his work as he always did after he had taken her home and the hours he put in had caught up with him, and he had overslept. That had been the morning when, arriving first, she had discovered she had left her keys at home and had gone round to the inexpensive flat where he lived.

He had come to the door with a hastily thrown on robe about him. And while she had stood there feeling excitement drumming through her veins that he didn't appear to have anything else on, he had exclaimed, 'Ye gods, is that the time!' and yanked her over the threshold, ordering her to make him coffee while he went and got dressed.

It was the first time she had been to his small flat. And because there was not enough room there in which to swing the proverbial cat, chasing to do his bidding, she had cannoned into him, and as he had spun round to save her from knocking into something solid, she had suddenly found herself in his arms.

'You smell gorgeous,' he had murmured, his face buried in her newly washed hair. And her heart danced a crazy rhythm as she had lifted her face for his kiss.

Though for one highly suspended moment she had thought he was not going to kiss her. Then a groan had broken from him, and heaven was hers, for his mouth was over hers, and as the heat of his body started to warm her, suddenly as she pressed to get nearer still to him, so, as another half-stifled groan left him, his kisses had thrilled her by changing and being different kisses from those kisses she had grown to know.

Desire for him was soon making itself felt in her. That same desire in him for her made her breathless as his hands had begun caressing her. Soon everything was forgotten between them, save that there was no need to stifle their need for each other, and Ellis took her with him to his bedroom. Sorrel knew then that she would have to be his, because it was what he wanted. For her part, never had she felt like this—she just had to have him too.

She had been sure then, as his hands had caressed her breasts, that she had his love. And, luxuriating in her full cup of happiness, she had stroked his shoulder as she had kissed his bare chest and breathed, 'I'm glad we don't have to wait until we're married.'

'Married!' Ellis had echoed, and with bewildering swiftness then his hands had left caressing her breasts to take her firmly by the shoulders.

But still she had smiled, not looking at him but guessing that with his business still not off the ground, he was about to tell her that he could not yet afford a wife.

'You won't need to pay me a wage when we're married,' she had gone blithely on, though she had then sensed that he was too proud to have her working for him for nothing. She was sure of it when abruptly he had brought her to sit up, his face stern and not at all that of the lover he had been.

'Listen to me, Sorrel,' he had begun sternly.

But she didn't want to listen to anything. She loved him, she was sure that he loved her, she wanted to be snuggled up close to him again, to feel his hair-roughened chest beneath her cheek again. She had smiled, she remembered, a warm giving smile, ready then, wanting then, to give him her all.

'If you don't want marriage straight away,' she had said, knowing sufficient of him to know that his work had to come first, 'then we'll wait. But,' shyly she had smiled, 'but I love you so much—you must let me come and live with you until then.'

'Live with me!' Ellis had exclaimed.

But she in her confidence had thought she had known what his exclamation had all been about. 'Oh, you're thinking of my parents, aren't you?' she had said, still smiling because nothing else mattered but that Ellis loved her and she loved him. 'They'll be stuffy about it, of course and ... and ...' she had gone shy again, but had overcome it to tell him brightly, 'and we'll have to try not to have babies until we're ...'

'Babies!'

It was his horror at the thought of babies that had finally got through to her that all was not as rosy as she had pictured it.

'D-don't you want babies?' she had asked.

Confirmation that he wanted neither marriage nor babies had been there in the way he had said harshly:

'Tidy your clothes, Sorrel, and get out of here.'

'Tidy ...?' she had echoed, her cheeks going scarlet as at last it had hit her that Ellis wanted none of what she was offering. But still she had to ask, 'Don't you—want me?'

'For God's sake will you get out!' he had roared, leaving the bed, finding her handbag on the floor and pushing it at her.

'But—I love you,' she had protested, staggered. 'You . . .'

'I,' he said, his face a chiselled mask by that time, 'have no room in my life for you.'

Had he slapped her, that blow could not have been more painful. But it had the desired effect. In minutes she had raced out of his flat. She barely remembered where she had gone that day; it certainly hadn't been back on the next bus to Salford Foley, nor had it been back to work to await Ellis's arrival with the key.

But her confidence, which had taken a severe blow, was to surface the next morning. Once again she had begun to believe that, from the many loving looks Ellis had sent her way, he must be in love with her.

Throughout the long fretful night she had puzzled at his attitude, until in the end she had at last seen just exactly where she had gone wrong. By that time, though Ellis had told her very little about his parents or his brother and sister, Sorrel was cursing herself for the idiot she had been to talk of babies. From what Ellis had let fall she had known that his father, a man with a keen brain, had been forced to let his ideas stagnate when, marrying early, his first responsibility had been to his wife and the three children who had arrived in quick succession.

The next day Sorrel had gone to work with it all planned out in her head. There would be no more talk of babies, or marriage either. She and Ellis would go back to the way they had been, and she would be content to let things go on that way until Ellis decided the business was sufficiently off the ground for him to do something about the love they had for each other.

Only it hadn't quite worked out that way. For, before she could so much as tell him that she would rather that

they forgot about yesterday, her startled eyes were to
see that there was another girl sitting at her typewriter.

And while she was getting over the shock of that, a
grim-faced Ellis was coming over to her and escorting
her outside and out of earshot of the new Girl Friday,
and he was gritting:

'I didn't expect to see you again.'

'You didn't . . .!' she gasped.

'I thought you'd realised yesterday that I no longer
need you,' he had told her toughly.

And inanely, to her everlasting shame, Sorrel clearly
remembered she had told him, 'But I love you, Ellis—I
always will.'

'Don't,' he had said tersely. 'You're wasting your
time,' and as a cutting afterthought, 'And mine,' he had
tossed at her, and had gone inside to leave her staring at
the door he had firmly closed to shut her out.

Somehow she had got home. But weeks had passed
with her still clinging on to the hope that Ellis loved
her. All hope had gone on the day she had heard that
he was dating Jenny Pearson, a girl from her village.
She had known then that Ellis had no regard for her
whatsoever. She had seen known then that she had imagined
all she had in those smiling looks, and that there had
been no sincerity in his love-filled glances. For,
knowing she would soon get to hear that he was dating
Jenny Pearson, never, if he had loved her, would Ellis
let her be hurt as that news had crucified her.

The months that followed that dreadful time when
her world had fallen apart were best forgotten. She had
suffered a breakdown, and only later did she realise
how supportive her strict parents had been in that they
did not badger her with questions, but let her live
through each day as best she was able.

Later it had been her mother who had seen the advert in the post office window that had announced that a nanny, previous experience unnecessary, was required by a lady in one of the big houses in the next village.

As she had trusted Ellis implicitly, Sorrel's faith in men was shattered. She had no wish to put herself in the position of repeating the bitter experience. To her mind then, children were by far the safer option.

So she had gone to look after the baby Arabella, and had learned in the next months to keep her sensitive emotions hidden. The Armitages, she had soon discovered, were a loose-living couple. And the way Leslie Armitage, as fickle as his wife for all he often appeared scared of her, went on did nothing to restore Sorrel's faith in the sincerity of men.

Often Sorrel would push baby Arabella to Salford Foley, and she was soon in receipt of all the news going. Jenny Pearson was no longer seeing Ellis Galbraith, but was going steady with some other man. Ellis, Sorrel heard, had left Kinglingham.

Over the next year she ceased looking for any redeeming light in the two adult Armitages. She was aware by then that the house belonged to Cynthia's father, though little comfort did he gain in his ailing years from having his daughter living with him. He was often ill, but because money went through her hands like water, the only time Cynthia went to sit by his bedside was when she wanted him to settle some of her outstanding bills.

With Cynthia openly telling Sorrel that, like a creaking gate, he could hang on for years and that she wasn't going to reduce her inheritance by paying a qualified nurse to wait on him, more and more of the responsibility for looking after him was placed on

Sorrel's shoulders. And by the time she had been working for the Armitages for four years and baby Benjamin had come along, she had grown so fond of the old man that she was in a position of knowing it would be 'God help him' if she left, because neither Cynthia nor Leslie cared a button about him.

A year after Benjamin was born, Cynthia cajoled her father into selling up so that they could all move to London. Knowing he hadn't got long, after much thought, for Mr Ollerenshaw's sake, Sorrel went with them. By then she was occasionally picking up a paper to see Ellis's face looking back at her. He was making it to the top.

She had been in London only a short while when she again saw his picture in the paper, this time with a stunning, sophisticated-looking blonde by the name of Wenda Sykes. Ellis was engaged to be married.

That he had not married Wenda was reported too, news of their broken engagement being more food for the newshounds. Time had gone on then, with Ellis having made it to the top, when it seemed to Sorrel that she couldn't pick up a paper without seeing a picture of him staring back at her—and always with some glamorous woman.

When Albert Ollerenshaw had died and had left her more money than she had ever seen in her life, Cynthia Armitage had been more furious than Sorrel had ever seen her.

'I've put up with having that old devil under my feet all these years and he dares to do this to me!' she had shrieked with rage when the news had been broken that because of her spendthrift ways her inheritance and that of the children was tied up so that she couldn't get her hands on it all at once. 'And you, you sneaky bitch,' she vent her spleen on Sorrel, 'not only has the old swine left you more than you'll ever earn in a lifetime—you can have yours straight away!' There had been more, much, much more. Language such as Sorrel had never heard had come spewing from the over-indulged woman. But the upshot of it all had been her shriek of, 'The old bastard wants you to "live a little", does he? Well, you can find somewhere else to live, for a start!'

The sound of a car door closing and Neville Drury saying his adieux to a departing guest had Sorrel blinking and coming away from her reverie to realise that for the first time in years she had been crying—and that not all her tears were on account of the passing of Albert Ollerenshaw.

CHAPTER TWO

SORREL had herself well in hand by the time she presented herself downstairs the following morning. Tears, she considered, were the privilege of adolescence, and anyway, what in goodness had she got to cry about? She had a nice home; money in the bank; and Rod Drury for an escort should she ever feel the need of masculine company.

Though she was not sure that she and Rod would not soon be parting company. If he looked at her very much more with that eager light in his eyes, it would leave her with no alternative but to bid him a permanent goodbye.

Sorrel's thoughts were interrupted when the Drurys' housekeeper appeared, to direct her to the breakfast room. 'The family have gone riding,' said Mrs Richards apologetically. 'Mr Roderick thought ...' she broke off, hesitating.

'He thought I might not surface before midday,' suggested Sorrel with a warm smile to put the housekeeper at her ease.

Perhaps rising at midday was what most sophisticated types did, she mused as Mrs Richards went away to prepare the coffee and toast she had requested. Though, regretfully, since she had worked hard on her new image, the habit of getting up at the crack of dawn to see to Arabella and Benjamin was so ingrained that Sorrel knew she would never be so sophisticated as to laze away a whole morning in bed.

Her breakfast soon disposed of, and not unhappy with her own company, she put on her sunglasses and wandered outside into the sunshine. She had no intention at all of thinking about Ellis Galbraith. But, when strolling across the lawn towards an old apple tree, she found she was wondering, but for that one never-to-be-forgotten occasion, if he still worked late and rose early. Putting him firmly from her mind, she made a conscious effort to concentrate on Rod, and what, if anything, she should do about him.

She had met Roderick Drury when she had needed legal advice about the lease on her flat. But once the legal matter was settled, he had turned up on moving-in day, to see, so he said, that everything was in accordance with the terms of her agreement. He had proved himself more than useful when he had stayed to fix a few plugs and put up a bracket or two. But he knew nothing of her previous circumstances. So far as he knew, she was a woman of independent means. And that was all he was going to know.

After Cynthia Armitage had dismissed her, she had returned to her parents' home for a few weeks. But she had been unable to settle, and had returned to London. To tell Rod anything of the threadbare bed-sitter she had moved into, or anything of the shop work she had taken while waiting for the slow working of his profession to finalise Mr Ollerenshaw's estate, would tell him too much about her. In her view, the less people knew about you, the less likely you were to form closer relationships, and to keep aloof from close relationships was the way she liked it. She had become a very private person.

Reaching the apple tree, Sorrel took off her sunglasses and sat herself down on the worn bench that seemed to have stood beneath the tree for as long as the house had stood.

The only close relationship she had, she reflected, was with her parents. It was funny how much her father had mellowed in recent years. Perhaps it was the responsibility of having a daughter to bring up that had made him the strict parent he had been in her growing years. He was more relaxed with her now at any rate, and she thought of it as a compliment to her that he had accepted that she was a person in her own right. Though both her parents were still very proud. They knew she had inherited some money, but beyond the acceptance of some pipe tobacco for her father and flowers for her mother whenever she returned to Salford Foley, they had determinedly refused to accept any financial gift from her.

Sorrel was just in the middle of thinking that maybe she would visit them again soon, when the sudden hurried beat of her heart told her that her eyes were not mistaken in that they had just spotted, and recognised, the tall casually dressed man who had just come from around the front of the house. He had spotted her too, and without altering his stride, he was making his way over to her.

In the shade of the apple tree, there was no need for her to don her sunglasses, but it was without obvious haste that she put them on. She had thought that when she and Rob returned to London that afternoon, it would be without her seeing Ellis Galbraith again.

By the time he had neared her bench, and without so much as a 'by your leave' had sat himself down beside her, Sorrel, her hair in an elegant knot, looking cool in her cream linen dress, had herself once more under control.

'The Drurys are all out riding,' she informed him, her voice unhurried, her manner easy.

She felt his eyes on her, and turned her head languidly, her heartbeats catching her out again as her green eyes feasted on that face that had once been so dearly familiar to her. That same hard jaw, that well remembered firm mouth—she looked at his dark eyes and the years fell away as she thought of how those eyes once crinkled in laughter.

That Ellis had no intention of looking from her, and did not like either that he could not read what was going on in her eyes, was evidenced by the short way he did no more than lift his hands to her face and remove her sunglasses,

'You don't need those,' he remarked. And while she fought a battle with a spurt of anger that would have ruined her cool front, he was advising her. 'I didn't come over to see the Drurys.'

'I'm honoured,' she drawled, not wanting to think that, by the sound of it, it was her he had come especially to see. 'That is—unless it's the downstairs maid you have your eye on.' Her eyes veiled, she saw the corner of his mouth twitch—but she didn't want him to be amused by anything she said either. In the old days they had always been idiotically grinning or smiling at some crack one or other of them had made. 'From what I hear, you have rather a reputation with women,' she added, thinking that might take the smile off his face.

It did. Though he was careless of his reputation, and was coming back with a deliberate, 'I prefer to use my eyes rather than listen to gossip.'

'Meaning?' she asked with a shrug that said she didn't care too much whether he answered her or not.

'Meaning that I'd have to be blind not to notice the change in you in the last eight years.'

She so nearly tossed him an uncaring 'Good heavens, has it been that long?'—but Ellis had always been pretty astute. There was, she considered, a grave danger, in her need to let him see how completely she had got over her love for him and those insincere looks of love he used to send her, that she might overplay her hand.

'Surely you didn't expect me to remain the same innocent child I was at seventeen?' she asked, a look of being slightly appalled on her face.

'At seventeen, your innocence was your most precious possession,' he replied shortly. 'Your freshness shone from you—it gave you an added beauty.'

'You never said,' she quipped in light sarcasm, and saw his mouth quirk again—only for it to shape into a tight line, as sharply he grunted:

'Did marriage do this to you?' And while she was coping with the shock that he thought she was married, he was going on in the same sharp tone, 'Never did I expect to bump into you the way I did last night, to sit at the same table with you and listen to you prattle on in a way that just isn't you.'

'You know nothing about me,' said Sorrel, her tone as sharp as his before she could stop it.

'I know that you obviously married money,' he retorted. Then, as suddenly, his manner was again relaxed, and quietly he was asking, 'What went wrong, Sorrel?'

'Wrong?' she queried, still trying to get over his insistence that she had somewhere along the way found it in her to trust some man enough to marry him.

'You aren't wearing a wedding ring.' His voice was

gentle when he asked, 'Did he give you a hard time? Did you divorce him?'

That gentle note weakened her when she did not want to be weakened. 'You think I've been married?' she asked, no sharpness in her as she went on, 'You think I've been through the divorce courts?'

His voice was sharp-edged again, his eyes hard on her as shortly he said, 'Haven't you?'

She looked from him, shaking her head, not seeing his reaction or knowing if indeed he had reacted at all, as she told him, 'I've never been married.'

A long silence stretched between them after that. Sorrel had been happy before Ellis had come and parked himself beside her. She wished he would go. She was starting to feel edgy when over the last six months life had gone placidly for her.

But, on the point of telling him that she wanted something from her room, before she could make her intended languid movement to get to her feet, she was again having to hold down a spurt of temper, when she heard that Ellis had the utter gall to ask suddenly:

'So what happened to you, Sorrel Maitland, after . . .'

She stopped him right there. 'After you sacked me?' she questioned, her control on her anger coming too late. Though she was in control again, when coolly she told him, 'I didn't, as you obviously expected, throw myself in the nearest river.' She even managed a smile, a flick of a glance at him, as she said, 'I grew up, Ellis.'

It was the first time in years that she had said his name. It had her feeling all choky inside. But in the way he had always been able to, Ellis made her want to smile, when, an eyebrow ascending, he drawled laconically:

'You've certainly done that.' His eyes went over her

figure. 'Your—shape—was quite something before, but . . .'

'You're *too* kind,' Sorrel murmured, and came so very near to joining in with his laugh, as again her sarcasm amused him, that she made that movement to stand up. 'If you'll excuse me,' she said politely, then felt her flesh begin to tingle when his hand came to her arm to stay her.

'Don't go yet,' he said. 'I haven't seen you in years.'

Sorrel had become adept in hardening her heart. 'Forgive me,' she said insincerely. 'But I received the impression, the last time we met, that if you didn't ever see me again, that would be all right with you.'

'My God, you've grown a hard edge,' he said shortly, his hand refusing to let go her arm. And, short with her still, angry with her, she thought, he barked the question, 'When did you stop laughing with your eyes?'

'I wasn't aware that I'd ever started,' she replied, liking the feeling of hate that stirred in her towards him, needing that hate when he would not let her go. But suddenly he was changing tack, and was bluntly asking:

'Do you intend to marry Rod Drury?'

'I'll think about it, and let you be the first to know,' she said smartly. She saw that this time he was not amused by her sarcasm. Though, having had just about enough of his questions about her and her life, and since she didn't want to ruin her image by an undignified tussle to get her arm free, she turned the tables on him, and just as smartly asked, 'What about you—didn't I read somewhere that you were once engaged?'

His look was thoughtful, and she guessed before she heard it that she wouldn't like what was coming. 'Been keeping tabs on me, Sorrel?' he had the nerve to ask.

She smiled, but it was an effort. 'You never used to be conceited,' she said acidly, and saw his eyes smile briefly at her charge before, all at once, those dark eyes went hard.

'I was engaged,' he said concisely. 'But it came to nothing.'

'Slip the noose, did she?' Sorrel's insincere smile was still there. But that was before, that hard look still about him, Ellis had her gripping hard on to the seat at the side of her, the side he could not see, when bluntly he replied:

'My financial position when I became engaged wasn't anywhere near what it is now. Wenda and I parted company when I discovered she was getting everything I couldn't give her—financially—by batting her eyelashes at some old boy with one foot in the grave.'

'She—married him?' asked Sorrel, but saw Ellis shake his head.

'She had no need—she'd done her work well. When he passed on, his fortune passed on to her—he left her everything.'

Sorrel hadn't inherited anywhere near a quarter of Albert Ollerenshaw's wealth. But in her view what he had left her still represented a fortune. It took her a deal of effort to make her voice sound cool and uncaring, as she said:

'You sound as if you have a down on any girl who might chance to be left something in an old man's will.'

'When there's no chance about it, it's disgusting,' he told her coldly. 'When Wenda latched on to that ailing old man, he didn't stand the smallest likelihood of seeing what she was after.'

'She—was kind to him, I expect,' said Sorrel, feeling sick inside.

'You can say that again,' he said grimly.

But Sorrel was surfacing from seeing that if Ellis ever knew how she had come by her own fortune, then he would instantly put her in the same money grasping category as his ex-fiancée.

'Sour grapes because you lost your love?' she found enough challenge to ask. But she heard that sour grapes had nothing to do with the stand Ellis had taken, when, looking entirely unconcerned, he dismissed her charge.

'When the old boy died, she had the impudence to seek me out.'

'But you told her what for?' Sorrel suggested—and, innocently, softly, she asked, 'Wenda wasn't your—er—secretary, was she?'

Ellis had never been slow on the uptake—he was not slow now. 'I didn't have to sack her,' he returned.

Looking away from those penetrating eyes that seemed to want to hold hers, she saw with relief that a jodhpur-clad Rod was just appearing through the French doors of the drawing room.

Languidly then, she rose to her feet. 'You do have the darndest luck with your women, Ellis,' she murmured—and had to be glad she had her back to him when his reply met her ears:

'You were never my woman, though, Sorrel, were you?'

Only by the skin of my teeth, she thought, and moved away. She met Rod halfway across the lawn and for the first time she was grateful that in his pleasure on seeing her, as he looked down into her face, Rod draped an arm across her shoulders.

A minute later she took a peep to the seat beneath the apple tree. Ellis was no longer there.

Rod Drury apologising profusely for not being there

when she had come down that morning made Sorrel
forget any thoughts that might have lingered about Ellis
Galbraith's expressed statement that he had not come
over to see the Drurys. That statement was confirmed
by the fact that he had not stayed around to greet any
of them when they had returned from exercising the
horses.

Lunch was a pleasant meal, with Sorrel more relaxed
than she had been yesterday. Moira Drury seemed
warmer too, so she could only guess that her stiff
attitude yesterday had rather put Rod's normally
warm-natured mother off.

Though with Rod sending Sorrel fond looks across
the table every now and again, she was beginning to
think that if his parents caught the way he looked at
her, they might start to get the idea that she was
something more to him than just a casual girl-friend.

To her discomfiture, this was borne out towards the
end of the meal. The wedding anniversary party Moira
and Neville were planning for a few weeks' time had
been the topic of conversation for some minutes when
Moira, perhaps reading correctly the signals her son's
eyes were giving her, promptly invited Sorrel down for
that weekend so she could join in the celebrations.

'It's very kind of you to ask me,' Sorrel replied, with
two very good reasons presenting themselves why she
would not be accepting the invitation. For one, this
short visit had shown her that Rod was more interested
in her than she had thought, and for the other she had
no wish whatsoever, since in all probability Ellis had
been invited to the party too, to see him again. 'But I'm
not sure if I'm free that weekend.' Her smile was
apologetic as she explained, 'I haven't brought my diary
with me.'

'If you remember,' Rod came in promptly, 'that's the weekend I asked you to keep free.' And with a disarming smile, 'I sort of guessed that once Mother had met you, she would want you to be part of the celebrations.' And while Sorrel's brain was rapidly trying to think up something that would not cause offence to either Moira or Neville, the smile Rod usually wore for her faded as he reproached, 'You did promise to keep those dates free, Sorrel.'

With three pairs of eyes on her, privately of the opinion that neither of his parents would miss her if she was not there, Sorrel's only option was to smile.

'Then I must have a blank space in my diary for that weekend,' she replied, and, her smile encompassing both Moira Drury and her husband, 'Thank you very much,' she said, 'I'd love to come.'

Her thoughts were broken into time and again on the drive back to London as Rod kept up a lively patter of conversation, in each brief lull, Sorrel was to grow more and more unsettled. In fairness she had to own that meeting Ellis Galbraith again had a lot to do with the way she was feeling. But it depressed her that by the look of it, Rod Drury was starting to become more attached to her than she wanted.

That he was an exceptionally nice man and would, she was sure, make some girl a wonderful husband one day, was all very well. Provided his thoughts weren't straying to believe that one day he might be acting that wonderful husband to one Sorrel Maitland.

She had seen enough unsound marriages in the set the Armitages belonged to, to know that in remaining single, she had missed nothing. And if the fraught marriage of Cynthia and Leslie Armitage had not been enough to put any girl off, she had a clear memory of Ellis in a rare confiding mood that had stupidly led her to believe he thought more of her than he actually did, telling her how his parents had been so much in love at the start of their marriage, but how they had ended up hating each other—their marriage had finished in divorce.

Rod Drury was pulling his car up outside her apartment block when, as she tried to think of anyone she knew who had stayed happily with the partner they had started out with; to contradict her thoughts that marriage brought nothing but strife, came the memory of not only how happy Rod's parents were together, but her own parents too.

As usual, when she had unlocked the outer door, Rod insisted on seeing her up to the door of her flat on the second floor. 'Do I get to come in for a few minutes?' he asked, his expression ever hopeful, causing her to wonder if now was the moment to tell him that she wasn't going to see him again.

The memory of the weekend at his parents' home she had committed herself to stopped her. She had virtually promised she would go, and she hated breaking promises.

'I'm rather tired,' she put him off his attempt to gain entry to her flat, where always talkative as he was, a few minutes would stretch into an hour before she would be able to close her door on him.

'All that fresh country air?' he suggested a shade wryly, seeming perfectly content to talk that hour away on her doorstep.

'It is rather enervating, isn't it?' she agreed solemnly.

'You never did tell me what Ellis Galbraith was doing sitting with you under the old apple tree this morning,' he said, bringing up a matter she had thought he had forgotten, since this was the first time he had referred to his coming back from the stables and seeing her with Ellis.

'Neither I did,' she said a shade coldly, to let him know that nobody put her through the third degree. But, as she saw the slightly taken aback look that came instantly to his face, she softened, and invented, 'He saw me sitting there when he was passing.' She shrugged. 'It was natural for him to come and say "Hello".'

'You used to live near each other, I think you said,' remarked Rod, in no hurry to go.

'That's right,' she answered, inserting her key into her door and hoping he would take the hint as she added easily, 'But that was years ago.'

Her door open, Sorrel stepped purposefully through the opening, and turned to bid him goodnight. But when Rod's face loomed close and he looked to be going to kiss her, as he had a few times before without her raising any objection, suddenly Sorrel could no more return his kiss than fly.

'Goodnight, Rod,' she said firmly, pulling her head out of range. 'Thank you for a lovely . . .'

'You enjoyed yourself?' he asked, while accepting that he wasn't going to get to kiss her, still in no hurry to go.

'Very much,' she replied, wanting to close the door.

'I'll call for you tomorrow,' he said, stepping back when she moved the door a few inches as though preparing to close it. 'I'll call about . . .'

'Tomorrow?' she asked.

'You haven't forgotten we're going to the first night of that new play?'

'Of course not,' she lied. 'I just wasn't thinking.'

She leaned heavily against the door when at last she had been able to close it on Rod Drury. She had thought herself unsettled coming home in his car, but, as her brow puckered, she wondered what had come over her a short while ago that, when his kisses before had meant nothing, had cost her nothing, she should suddenly be visited by an aversion to being kissed by him or any man.

Without prompting, all at once into her mind came the memory of how eagerly she had once welcomed Ellis's mouth on hers. How joyously she had thrilled to having his arms around her.

She came away from the door banishing the picture of the innocent seventeen-year-old she had been, but only for another thought to come and trip her up. That thought—would she be averse to Ellis's kisses too, should he ever want to kiss her again?

Not that he would want to kiss her, she thought, starting to feel fed up. Not that she would let him. He might have remembered the girl she had been at seventeen with a clear memory of her freshness, but if her instinct was right, very clearly he had no liking for the woman she had turned into at twenty-five.

She went into her bedroom and sat down before her dressing table mirror. Solemnly she stared at her delicate features. If she was truthful, she mused, her phoney air of sophistication gone, she wasn't sure that she liked what she had become very much herself either.

CHAPTER THREE

Awake early after only a fitful night's sleep, Sorrel got out of bed the next morning no happier with herself than she had been when she went to bed.

She went over to her wardrobe and pulled the doors wide trying to decide what to put on. But on discarding first one fine garment and then with dissatisfaction another, the cost of which had made her blink at the time, she remembered, she discovered that her expensive clothes meant nothing to her.

Settling for wearing what she felt most comfortable in, her jeans from her old days and a much washed T-shirt, she was then posing herself the question—why on earth had she spent all that money on a new wardrobe if she was happier grubbing around in casual gear?

The answer that suddenly appeared out of the blue was to shock her and make her collapse into a chair. Minutes later, having faced facts with an honesty she could wish was not a part of her, Sorrel was still gasping at the appalling truth that confronted her. Entirely without being aware of it, what she had done had been to turn herself into a near enough carbon copy of the sort of female she had seen pictured on the arm of Ellis Galbraith so many times!

Astonished, as vivid and clear recollection came to her of his ex-fiancée Wenda Sykes, she knew then that her sophisticated pose had nothing at all to do with her trying to comply with what old Mr Ollerenshaw had instructed in his will. It had nothing to do with his request that she 'live a little', she saw. At the very root of her leasing this expensive flat and making believe she was something she was not, was a desire to be the type of woman Ellis Galbraith so obviously admired!

Rocked to her foundations, Sorrel took about half an hour to surface from her amazing discovery. Her first instinct then was to set to straight away and do something about it.

But that instinct was to take second place when it came to her how well her air of sophistication had served her when she had bumped into Ellis again. For with her cool detached air well out in front, not only Ellis but Rod Drury and his parents too had espied nothing of the inner turbulence that had filled her.

Her mind was a mixture then of, should she return to the clothes-careless girl she had been, or should she, for the moment, stay with the protective mantle she had adopted? Her telephone rang before she had reached any conclusion.

It was not yet half past eight, so Sorrel hoped her caller was not going to be Rod Drury ringing to remind her that he was taking her to the theatre that night. Though remembering how he seemed to think she never surfaced until the sun was high in the sky, she changed her mind that it might be him as she went to answer the phone.

To hear Ellis Galbraith's deep-timbred voice the moment she had given her number made her almost drop the instrument. But aggression, against him, against the recent discovery about herself, was suddenly there to get her through the next few minutes.

'How did you get my number?' she demanded sharply, not trying to disguise that she was not, to put it mildly, very pleased about it.

'With difficulty,' Ellis replied, and paused—but added when that obviously wasn't enough for her, 'First I had to ring Rod Drury.'

'Rod Drury gave it to you!' she exclaimed.

'Under protest, I think,' said Ellis, a smile in his voice. Though his voice was even when he said, 'He also staked proprietorial rights by telling me that he's taking you to the theatre tonight.' And before Sorrel was sure how she felt about that remark, his voice even still, Ellis was asking, 'Has he a proprietorial right, Sorrel?'

'That's none of your damned business!' she flared, drawing breath to tell him more in the same vein. Only she did not get the chance.

'Which means he hasn't,' Ellis chopped her off before she was ready. And, with the cheek of the very devil, she thought, he said, 'Come out with me.'

'I did that when I was seventeen,' she said angrily, and had put down the phone on him before she had time to think about it.

Inwardly groaning, wishing she hadn't said that bit about when she was seventeen, Sorrel hated him because her stupid remark might have given him some inkling as to how desperately she had been hurt by him at seventeen.

Damn him, she thought, pacing the floor, why did he have to come back into her life? She was over him, cured. Nothing had had the power to upset her since she had got over him. Not Cynthia Armitage's vile insults, or even dear old Mr Ollerenshaw dying, had seen her in the state she was in now. Her hands shaking, her insides a turmoil from just that phone call, Sorrel damned Ellis Galbraith again.

By the time evening came and she was dressed in a full-length green silk dress, she was once more in charge

of her person. Calmly then she was able to greet Rod
when he called for her, taking his usual compliment to
her beauty in her stride.

'Hope the play's up to scratch,' he commented when
they were settled in their seats. 'But just in case we're in
need of some lighter entertainment, I've booked a table
at a night club for later.'

'Lovely,' murmured Sorrel, trying to find some
enthusiasm. A few minutes later the curtain went up
and the play began.

It was a good play, and knowing that the tickets had
been like gold to obtain, Sorrel tried to lose herself in
the top quality of the acting. But, owning to feeling
fidgety inside, she was again hating Ellis Galbraith that,
after all this time, his sudden appearance back in her
life had disturbed her far more than it had any right to.

Heartily sick and tired of him forever popping
uninvited into her mind, she felt it was just about the
last straw when they adjourned during the interval, Rod
leaving her to go to the bar, and Ellis Galbraith was
about the first person she saw.

He seemed to stand out from everyone else at any
rate. Tall, dark and distinguished in his well cut clothes,
there was an unpretentious air of arrogance about him
as he surveyed the crowded mass, each hoping to relieve
their thirst before time ran out and they had to return
to their seats.

Not short in stature herself, Sorrel was glad of a large
man in front of her who afforded her the chance of
observing Ellis without being seen herself as he started
to move from where he had been standing.

Remembering his impertinent 'Come out with me,'
she wondered, ridiculously, she owned, had he
deliberately come to the theatre that night because he

had known that she would be there? Truly ridiculous, she was telling herself a second later, because the play had been sold out ages ago, which had to mean Ellis had been in possession of his ticket long before today.

Her heart started to pump energetically when from her vantage point she saw that it was in her direction that he was heading. For one wild moment, panic-stricken, she almost took to her heels. Then to the left of her, somebody addressing a woman whom she hadn't had time to notice as 'Wenda' had her eyes leaving Ellis to go to the stunning girl nearby, who was none other than the girl he had once been engaged to!

A painful stab of jealousy she was unprepared for caught her out that Ellis had not the slightest interest in coming to say 'hello' to her, but that it was his ex-fiancée he was coming over to see, despite his suggestion that he had told her where to get off.

But, still thinking she was hidden from his view, what happened in the next few moments was to leave her feeling temporarily numb of all sensation; then fighting hard to stay cool and make it appear that she was totally unaffected.

For, reaching a point where if he turned to the right he would be going over to greet his ex-fiancée, so as she heard Wenda's sultry-voiced call of, 'Hello, Ellis,' so Sorrel saw that Ellis had not even seen Wenda. And, if she could believe her eyes, she saw a look that was so contemptuous of the woman he had once been engaged to in his eyes that she just knew that it would not bother him if he never saw Wenda again. Though the moment before he turned to the left and in her direction, his good manners did manage to surface sufficiently for him to nod a curt, if civilised, greeting to the woman he once must have loved.

Shaken, Sorrel knew then that Ellis's disgust with Wenda because she had been 'kind' to some old man with a foot in his grave for her own ends had been no false statement. And as feeling began to course through her again, at that moment she knew that she personally would never survive should Ellis ever get to hear about her own kindness to an ailing old man, and the money he had left her, and in consequence, serve her with so much as a sample of that same disgusted, withering contempt.

She was to be never more glad of her sophisticated front when, either having seen her all along, or having only just spotted her waiting there for Rod to come back, Ellis stopped dead in front of her. The contempt had left his eyes, she saw, admiration replacing it as he took in the polished look of her in her pale green silk.

'You're a long way from home,' she managed to find her voice, and even compliment herself on the affected sound of it.

Ellis's right eyebrow arched upwards a fraction at her tone, but his voice was level as he replied, 'I have a flat in town.'

Appearing to take that in her stride, Sorrel managed to remain cool, treating this meeting as accidental, as she was now sure it was, she asked:

'What do you think of the play so far?' and wanted to hit him for not playing according to the rules, when he said:

'I prefer one conversation at a time. We haven't finished the conversation we started this morning yet.'

Indifferently, she shrugged. 'I thought we had,' she drawled, for all the world as though his phone call, his asking her to go out with him, had had as little effect as that.

She wasn't surprised that her manner irritated him. She saw from the slight narrowing of his eyes that he didn't care much for her attitude. But, when she was convinced that not one more word would he stay to address to her, all at once he was pulling his head back and was thoughtfully surveying her. Then, his even tone gone, he was saying:

'I just don't believe this.'

Without thinking first, Sorrel went plunging in to ask, 'You don't believe—what?'

His eyes fixed on hers, refusing to let her look away, his expression severe, unhesitatingly Ellis told her, 'This isn't the real you, Sorrel Maitland.'

Of all the people she knew, Ellis was the last person she wanted to see straight through her. But when the thought struck that once she had been so open with him, her mind such an open book to him that he more than anyone else should know what made her tick; she felt angry that he had been uncaring of her in the past, so what the hell was it to him now how she acted.

Affecting a light sophisticated laugh, she looked him fully in the eyes, as she tinkled, 'It's the only me I have, Ellis.' She was glad again of that anger, when, slicing through her affectation, quietly, his voice gentle, Ellis dared to ask:

'Did I do this to you, Sorrel?'

She had to look away from him then, her teeth clenching hard as she fought for control at the nerve of him. From the corner of her eye, she saw Rod coming away from the scrum over by the bar.

'Your conceit is showing again, Ellis,' she said at last. And, proud of her control, she even managed another look at him, before, her head that inch or two higher, she left him and went towards Rod.

She made the crush of people her excuse that her shaking hands slopped a few drops of the drink she took from Rod. But even as Rod was commenting that he had seen her talking to Ellis, Sorrel recognised why it was she was shaking so inside. Many things she had remembered about Ellis, but one of the things she had forgotten until now was that light of battle that would come into his eyes when, loving a challenge, he took up that challenge. If she wasn't very much mistaken, that light that said he was metaphorically rolling up his sleeves for a fight had come into his eyes in that moment of her turning and walking so loftily away from him!

Throughout the remainder of that evening Sorrel spent many moments in telling herself that she *had* been mistaken. That even if Ellis had asked her for a date and had been refused, since she meant so little to him in the past, he was man enough to accept that not all the women of his acquaintance were waiting with bated breath for him to ask them out.

Determined to oust Ellis from her thoughts, she was warmer to Rod than she had meant to be. And that Rod seemed to like it was evidenced in the many times he smiled at her as they danced, and dined, and chatted away.

But the evening stretching endlessly, which was all right by her since she had no wish to go to bed, when having thought she had successfully rid herself of thoughts of Ellis, Rod undid all her good work by bringing his name up when referring to his having telephoned him for her number.

Inwardly despairing, Sorrel kept a smile on her face, her powers of invention sometimes brilliant, she owned, as without turning a hair she told Rod:

'He could have saved you and himself the trouble,' and smiling still, she explained, 'He wanted the address of a mutual acquaintance in Wiltshire—had he been sure in advance that we would bump into each other at the theatre tonight, he could have saved himself a phone call.'

Regardless that it had been past two in the morning when Rod took her home, he would again not have minded had Sorrel invited him in for a 'minute or two'.

But he knew it was not on the cards, as with a smiling, 'Thank you for a lovely evening,' she inserted her key into the door of her flat.

'Are you doing anything tomorrow?' he asked, not one to let the grass grow.

'Call me,' she invited, as she again avoided his lips by bidding him, 'Goodnight, Rod.'

It seemed to Sorrel that she had only just closed her eyes when there was a knocking at her door to awaken her. Still half asleep, she opened her eyes to see from her clock that it was half past eight.

Not surprised to find, since she had slept only fitfully the night before, and had only been in bed a few hours since Rod had brought her home, that she had slept past her usual waking up time, she dragged herself out of bed and wrapped a robe about her. Her mind was still sluggish as she went to see who was calling in what seemed to her, in her still half asleep head, to be the middle of the night.

To see a business-suited Ellis Galbraith standing there, a hint of a smile on his mouth as he witnessed the pink bloom of being newly awakened on her, her thick sunkissed hair out of the knot in which she wore it these days, and cascading in a tumble of tousled waves about her shoulders, had the same effect as if she had just splashed her face in cold water.

'What . . .' she gasped, and was speechless for a moment, until, not waiting to be invited, Ellis did no more than put her to one side, when he calmly stepped over her threshold and closed the door. 'What the . . .' she began again, and having on the instant built up a full head of steam, 'How did you get in?' she demanded. 'And what,' she fired, her sophisticated image nowhere to be seen, 'do you mean by waking me when I was fast asleep?'

Unaware of how attractive she looked with her robe thrown carelessly about her, the blaze of fire in her eyes, she was not made any sweeter when, his eyes lingering over her, Ellis took his time before he answered.

'One of the other residents let me in on his way out.' And his eyes still on her, he had the insolence to remind her of how, in her eagerness to get to work in the old days, she used to catch the seven-thirty bus. 'In the old days you used to get out of bed with the birds.'

'This isn't . . .' she started to flare—but she broke off abruptly when he glared at her with a look of sudden and unpremeditated fury. And, while bewildered that his expression was all at once threatening murder, she was to stand open-mouthed as Ellis moved and she heard him roar:

'Or were you not in bed *alone*?'

Her eyes like saucers, she saw him stride past her; and go storming in search of her bedroom! Her disbelieving eyes following him, Sorrel was having to believe that in his amazing audacity, he was checking for himself to see if indeed she had slept alone!

The utter nerve of him had her recovering, to be as instantly furious as he had been. Spluttering with rage, she chased after him. 'What the hell do you think you're doing?' she yelled when, not a yard separating them, she found him looking at her empty bed.

As quickly as it had come, his fury drained from him, and she saw a muscle jerk in his jaw. A moment later he was growling, 'God knows.' And in the next moment, just as though she hadn't already had enough shocks since she had opened her eyes, Ellis was reaching for her and was pulling her into his arms.

The bliss that having his arms around her would have afforded, if she let it, was not to be thought of, and Sorrel was having to fight with all she had to stay angry. For Ellis was making no attempt to kiss her—though that, she thought agitatedly, did not mean that he might not do so before he was finished. But she could not allow that.

She gave a heave to get herself free, but on finding that that proved useless, for he still held her firmly to him, she was left with having to try to shock those arms from around her.

'If it's your intention to rape me, Ellis Galbraith, then damn well get on with it!' she said heatedly. 'If not, then clear off!'

She knew he was laughing even before she got to the end. His laughter was unexpected. But what was even more unexpected was that she should see the funny side of it too.

She was still in his arms when, laughter bubbling up inside her, she looked up to see his mirth-filled face. She could not hold it in; laughter, natural laughter, was forcing her lips apart, and had burst beyond her control from her, curving her mouth upward as she looked at him.

Her heart drumming, her laughter as suddenly fell away from her as she felt a sudden fear, with Ellis looking into her eyes, he might see more than she would want him to see. Quickly she dipped her head. But weakness was attacking her, and for long moments, their laughter done with, she just could not find the strength to obey her head and again attempt to get away from him. But I must, said that desperate voice within her, and she had found that moment of strength to push at him.

For her pains, Ellis's arms tightened fractionally about her. 'Let me hold you for a moment,' he murmured, his tone soothing, making her too weak as her strength left her just then to endorse her 'clear off' statement with another push at him.

Her limbs like so much water, she leant against him. More weakness invaded her when she felt the touch of his lips against her hair and the breath of his, 'Your hair smells the way it always did,' just as though he had never forgotten the fragrance, as his hands warmed her skin through the material of her robe.

How long she stood like that within the circle of his arms, mindless of anything, with no thought in her head of the brokenhearted struggle it had been to recover from his rejection of her before, she had no idea. But it was Ellis's timely reminder of the heartbreak she had endured when he said softly to the top of her head, 'You're still the girl I used to know, aren't you, Sorrel?' that she came rapidly away from his seduction of her senses.

Her body stiffened in his hold and the cold look of her as she raised an unsmiling face, made him loosen her from his embrace.

Smartly she took a step away from him. 'You're wrong, Ellis,' she told him, no heat in her. But he was shaking his head to contradict her before she had finished.

'Don't lie to me—you never used to,' he reminded her, which she saw must weaken his argument in that she must have changed if she could lie to him now when she had never done so in the past. 'The girl I used to know would smile, laugh with her eyes before that smile had time to reach her mouth. You did it again just now,' he said. 'You laughed with me, and not five minutes ago showed me that you're still the same Sorrel you used to be.'

She took another step from him. Her peace of mind when he had gone demanded that she get through to him that there was no trace in her now of the trusting teenager she had been.

But all her reserves were called upon before she had the strength to look at him again. Before she could find the cool sophisticated manner she wanted to be able to tell him coldly:

'I'm no longer the girl who made such a fool of herself over you.' He looked set to argue still, she saw, and she moved in swiftly then to tell him, 'Nor would I want to be, Ellis.'

That stopped him. His eyes never more serious, he stood where he was, his eyes never leaving her face. She thought that he was still going to argue, but then suddenly his stern expression left him, and his face was breaking in less severe lines, when quietly the question left him:

'I hurt you very badly, didn't I?'

Sorrel was becoming more and more practised in the offhand shrug; she put in some more practice as she lied, 'I was over that years ago.' To her mind, then, it was more than time that Ellis went on his way.

She made her intention of seeing him out obvious by turning from the bedroom and moving towards her flat door. Whether Ellis had had any particular reason for calling and getting her out of bed she neither knew nor cared any longer. She wanted to be by herself. Or more precisely, she wanted him out of her flat, and out of her life where up until a few days ago she had thought he safely was.

A slight surprise touched her when without further argument, Ellis moved to stand near her. What was going on behind those dark depths of his eyes, she had no way of knowing. But she could be sure that it wasn't from any feeling of sensitivity for her and the pain he had caused her in the past that he was leaving.

Though, when it looked as though he would go without so much as another word, as she left the door he turned, his voice light and easy, as he made the offer:

'I'll hang on and give you a lift to your office.'

Silently, Sorrel looked at him, not moving as she took in the fact that he plainly thought she had continued in secretarial work after he had sacked her, and that he thought she had brought her office skills to London.

Though when she had neither gone to bathe and get dressed, and in fact had not moved so much as one step, his easy look disappeared. She saw the way his eyes narrowed as, knowing she came not from moneyed people, he looked round the room and took in her expensive furnishings. She was not surprised when she saw the glint of dark suspicion come into those all-seeing eyes.

'With the sort of job you must have,' he commented after several still moments, 'you most likely run your own car.'

He was giving her all the time she needed to answer. But when she had said not one word to confirm the

suspicion that was growing in him, his voice sounded
tough when he asked, 'Do I need to give you a lift to
your office?'

Sorrel had been looking for a way to get him out of
her life. But now that she had that way, she found that
the words to end their re-acquaintance were not so easy
to part with.

'I—do have a car,' she told him at last, her head
coming up, ready for his suspicious mind to quickly
find any answers outstanding. 'But I don't have a job to
go to.'

Ice was there in an instant. His face had gone hard as
he clipped, 'Who pays for all this?' And, not waiting for
her to tell him, 'Drury?' he charged angrily.

'No,' she said sharply. But, remembering the
contempt she had seen in his eyes for Wenda Sykes only
last night, she would not in any case have told him
about old Mr Ollerenshaw. 'In fact,' she said, and
wanting him out of there, she went past him to hold the
door wide, 'the man who pays for—my life style—is no
one you know.'

It was ten o'clock before Sorrel found the energy to
go and get showered and dressed. Ellis had gone on his
way despising her that he thought she was some man's
kept woman—how much more he would despise her if
he knew where the money for her expensive apartment
and all its trappings had come from!

That she was having to face the fact that she still
loved Ellis, and was doubtful now that she had ever
stopped loving him, was something she had tried to
avoid ever since she had walked into the Drury's
drawing room a few nights ago.

And that was the reason she had had to make sure
that Ellis did not phone her or call at her flat to see her

ever again. He might have had his mind on some small dalliance with her, but, remembering how her heart had pounded to be in his arms not two hours ago, she knew that he must again be cut out of her heart. Never again could she let him get close to her. It had wrung her dry to get over him before. She could not bear to go through all that trauma again, all that hurt. She just couldn't face it. To be rejected by him a second time would destroy her.

CHAPTER FOUR

WHEN first one week went by and then another since that morning when Ellis had walked out of her flat, so any lingering touch of fear in Sorrel that she might answer her door or phone to find it was him slowly dwindled and finally died.

As she had suspected, Ellis had no time for her now he thought she must have some wealthy lover. No doubt he had decided too that, since she lived alone, her lover must be a married man whom she only saw when he could get away from his wife. Well, that, to her way of thinking, was all right by her. She didn't want Ellis forever contacting her when least expected—she would never have a chance to forget him that way.

Though in the two weeks that followed that morning when for a few moments he had held her in his arms, she was to find that her head was so full of him that she had done nothing about discarding the life style she now found alien. Nor had she found time to think very deeply about what she was going to do about Rod Drury. And that she was going to have to do something about Rod had been borne in on her more and more recently by the odd remark here and there, and by those unwanted warm glances he would send her way.

Sorrel was getting ready to go to some party or other with Rod that night when, finding herself selecting any dress at random, the party having so little meaning for her, she suddenly realised that she would just as soon not go.

It was at that point of giving herself a mental shake, that she realised too that she was just not being fair to Rod. True, she had not asked him to grow fond of her. But, having no wish to hurt his feelings, she had done very little save ward off the moments lately when he would have taken her in his arms, to discourage him.

To recognise then that Ellis was the reason she could no longer allow Rod to kiss her on parting, made her try to drum up hate against the man who held her heart. For it was only since his brief reappearance in her life that something inside her had thought to object that any other man should lay claim to her mouth.

But, her word given, committed as she saw it to going to the party with Rod, she determined right there and then that when he brought her home that night, she would tell him she was not going to see him again.

It was a relief to have the decision made—even if part of that relief did stem from knowing if she told Rod what she had to tell him, it would mean, whether she liked breaking promises or not, that promise to attend his parents' wedding anniversary celebrations would be nullified. For neither Rod nor his parents would expect her to attend if she was no longer going out with him.

Everything settled in her mind, the chance of bumping into Ellis again neatly done away with since she would not be anywhere near the Drury's home next Friday, Sorrel finished getting ready, and sat down to await Rod's arrival.

As usual, he was early, his compliments profuse as he observed her in her amber-coloured dress. 'I'm going to be the envy of every man there tonight,' he said proudly, not asking him to come in, Sorrel secured her flat door behind her.

'Will there be many people there?' she asked, more to

take his attention away from herself than from any particular interest.

'The world and his wife, I shouldn't wonder,' he replied, setting the car in motion. 'The Fentons don't go in for small parties, but usually have one big one where they return in one go all the hospitality they've received throughout the year.'

'It sounds fun,' said Sorrel, good manners decreeing that she show some enthusiasm.

As Rod had suggested, the house of Lilian and Vernon Fenton was crammed to the seams. Sorrel found the Fentons a likeable couple, but with the hosts keeping an eye on things, and with so many people moving in and out from the main room to the buffet room and upstairs to where a couple of bedrooms were doing duty as cloakrooms, an informal atmosphere prevailing, it was only for a short while that she and Rod had any sort of conversation with them.

With most of the talk being only the surface sort, Sorrel found the next couple of hours passing pleasantly enough. She had danced, and she had chatted, but if her whole heart wasn't really in it, then she was the only one who knew it.

Rod had introduced her to several people, and they were in idle conversation with four other people, when one of the women who had been introduced as Beverly, after a flicked glance to the door, suddenly made the aside to the other female with them:

'Trust dear Cynthia to forget she's pushing forty, and leave it late enough to try and make an entrance!'

There had been no love lost in Beverly's voice. But when Sorrel's eyes, like the rest of the group, went to the door, so any enjoyment she had experienced rapidly departed.

A sick feeling hit the pit of her stomach as her eyes followed Cynthia Armitage already separating from her husband, her loud cry of, 'Darling!' as she kissed and greeted the nearest man, clearly to be heard above the buzz of conversation in the room.

As yet, Sorrel saw that Cynthia seemed in no hurry to go on to the next knot of people, but she knew Cynthia of old. Should she come anywhere near to where she was standing, then regardless of the fact that they were both guests in someone else's home, that would not stop her from making a scene.

'I can't stand this,' Beverly announced suddenly, Cynthia's penetrating voice getting on her nerves, apparently. 'Let's go and get something to eat.'

'Hungry, Sorrel?' asked Rod attentively. And at her statement that she wouldn't mind a bite, the six of them ambled through to the buffet by way of another door.

What Beverly had against Cynthia Armitage, Sorrel never learned. For it was out of sight, out of mind as far as Beverly was concerned when, after a sortie to the buffet table, they joined up again, for conversation again became light and general, with none of them of a mind to return to the other room.

'Midnight,' said Beverly all at once.

And as her husband burst out laughing and explained on her behalf, 'We're not going home by pumpkin, Bev has an early morning date with a set of golf clubs,' amid farewells as two of their number departed, Sorrell saw that Rod looked as though he wouldn't mind being on his way either.

Suspecting that he might have a case he wanted to put in a few hours on early tomorrow morning, she had no objection to following the lead set by Beverly and her husband.

'Shall we go too?' she suggested, and received quite a loving smile from Rod that she had read his mind.

They said their goodbyes to the couple they were with, and meeting their host and hostess in the hall, were able to give their thanks for a splendid party without the need to go and look for them. Then, with Rod waiting at the foot of the stairs, Sorrel went up to the bedroom where she had left her wrap.

Though if she had hoped to leave the party without being embroiled in a scene with Cynthia Armitage, the moment Sorrel entered the bedroom and saw her there holding court with two other women, she knew that her luck had just run out.

Cynthia's face went livid the moment she saw her, and all Sorrel's hopes of retrieving her wrap and of leaving without a word being exchanged went up in smoke as, 'My God—you!' her ex-employer screeched.

She then seemed lost for words, but it was for only a second that peace reigned. For as Sorrel had known she would, she welcomed an audience and was soon laying her tongue to every name she could, while the two other women looked on. Her vindictiveness knew no limits that a mere nanny should be moving in the same exalted circles as herself, as she went on to regale her listeners with the story of how 'this conniving bitch had conned her beloved father into leaving her money in his will.'

'Every last rag she has on her back has been bought with money that should be mine,' she ranted on, her spiteful eyes making a meal of Sorrel's amber dress.

Nowhere near as calm as she was trying to appear, Sorrel spotted her stole and caught hold of it. She was sorely tempted, as anger hit, to tell Cynthia Armitage a few home truths. Her friends might be wearing a different look on their faces were she to tell them that Cynthia had been so ashamed of her father and his dropped aitches that if she could have found an easier way to wheedle money to constantly top up her bank account, then no way would she have lived under his roof.

But she restrained the impulse, turning her back on the small satisfaction that would have been hers to reveal how Cynthia would have left her father to starve the sooner to get her hands on her inheritance. That it had been she who had tried to tempt his appetite in those last months of his life, not his daughter. Sorrel turned her back on Cynthia too, who hadn't finished telling yet about how her poor dear darling father had been sucked up to ... As quietly as she had entered, Sorrel left the room.

Rod, without knowing it, was a calming influence on the way home. For since he knew nothing of what had gone on upstairs, his conversation was on matters away from the party. Not that Sorrel could put that scene from her mind so completely, and she was only half with Rod as part of her went on to wonder if it would have been better to have stayed and, nauseating though it would be, had a slanging match with Cynthia Armitage. It was obvious that Cynthia's venom had not lessened. And the fact that she had walked out and frustrated any further attempt to belittle her in front of people had left Cynthia with still plenty to say should they ever meet at some other party.

Half wishing then that she had stayed to let Cynthia get all the spite out of her system, Sorrel came away from her thoughts to see that they had reached her flat. And it was only when Rod escorted her into her apartment building and she felt his arm come around her shoulders that she saw that she should have been spending that time on the car ride home in sorting through for the best way to tell him that this was the last time she was going to see him.

Going up in the lift afforded barely any time for her to get her thoughts together, and they were at the door of her flat when, before she could so much as get the first word out, Rod was forestalling her by suddenly saying:

'I'm glad you wanted to leave the party when I did.'

An ominous feeling started to creep over her that, from the tense look of him, she had left what she had to say to him a little too late!

'It was a—good party, wasn't it,' she said, hoping she was wrong with the suspicion that had just come to her, for never had she seen him looking so intent, so serious.

'I wanted to bring you home early so that you wouldn't be too tired to listen to what I have to tell you—to ask you,' he said, to her despair.

'Rod, I . . .' she began, trying to head him off. But Rod, she was to hear, was not to be headed off.

'You must know that I love you,' he went on. And while something inside her froze that she was going to have to hurt him, he was continuing quickly, 'Do I get to come in so that I can ask you to marry me?'

'Rod . . .' Helplessly Sorrel paused, but her expression was telling him more than she knew. For his face had fallen before quietly, she could get to tell him, 'Rod, I'm—sorry.'

There was no need now to tell him that she was not going to see him again, because although he tried to deny the answer he could see in her eyes, in that quiet 'I'm sorry' he just had to know that there was no future for the two of them together.

'Don't say anything,' he told her in a sudden rush. 'Think about it for a while. You might like the idea once you get used to it,' he pressed hurriedly. But Sorrel was shaking her head.

'I can't marry you,' she said gently. And since there was no way she could take the sting out of her next words, 'I'm sorry,' she said again. 'I like you so very much, Rod, but I don't love you.'

'You might learn to love . . .' he tried, but again she was shaking her head.

'I won't, Rod,' she said, with such certainty in her voice that he sucked in a short breath, then asked:

'Are you in love with somebody else?'

Caught out, Sorrel might admit to herself where her heart lay, but pride demanded that no one else knew of her unrequited love.

'No, I'm in love with no one,' she lied.

'Then marry me,' he urged promptly. 'We get on well, and . . .'

'No, Rod,' she cut him off. And because it was true, honestly, she told him, 'I don't want to marry anyone.'

It was the honesty in her eyes that came with what she had just said that seemed to convince him he was banging his head against a brick wall. But Sorrel felt sad when, without saying another word, he just bent his head and saluted her cheek with a kiss, and not in a mind to wait for the lift, went quickly towards the stairs.

Sorrel watched him until he had gone from her sight, not inserting the key into her door until she had heard the outer door lock behind him. To her, just then, it seemed less of a harsh dismissal if she waited until he was clear of the building before she closed her flat door on him.

But, her heart was heavy as she realised that, although she had not set out to deliberately hurt him, hurt him she had—but the hurt left her the moment she had the door of her flat open. For a sound to the left of her, just before she crossed her threshold, made her turn her head, her eyes going enormous to see, stepping from around the corner where he had been hidden, none other than—Ellis Galbraith!

Gaping, incapable of speech, so great was her shock that Ellis had actually pushed her inside her flat and come in with her before she had recovered sufficiently to decide to write to whoever it was one wrote to about the security, or rather the lack of it, in the building, she scarcely had enough wind to blaze:

'How did you get in?'

That she was going to have to whistle for her answer became plain, as, not one iota put out that she appeared ready to physically throw him out, Ellis smiled a smile she had no belief in, as he murmured:

'So friend Drury is out of luck!' And while she was gaping afresh that not only had he, by the sound of it, unashamedly listened and heard every word of Rod's proposal—and his being turned down—as cool as you like, Ellis's mouth quirked again, though more naturally this time as he asked, 'Going to make me a cup of coffee?'

'Coffee!' she repeated, her eyes going wide at the sheer audacity of him. 'Like hell I'll make you coffee!' she added as she started to recover. And at his look that said 'Now is that nice?' all her instincts of self-preservation rose to the surface as though to try and contradict how alive she felt just to have him there. 'It's late, and I'm tired,' she told him snappily.

Briefly her disquiet began to fade when it looked as

though Ellis was going to heed her not too subtle hint that he should leave. 'All right,' he said, a resigned look coming to his features. But her relief was shortlived. For he turned from her, but not towards the outer door. 'I'll make it,' he said, and was already heading to where her kitchen lay. 'Would you like one?' he thought to ask.

On the one hand wanting to thump him for his sheer unmitigated nerve, in spite of herself Sorrel's sense of humour decided at that moment to come out of hiding. She tried hard to stay cross with him, and was sure she didn't like him very much when, just as her mouth picked up at the corners, he turned back again.

Not wanting him to see any lingering traces of the Sorrel she had been who had been ready to laugh at the smallest crack he made, she moved to turn away.

'I don't take sugar,' she said grumpily, accepting his offer to make her a cup of coffee while he was making his own, though expecting some sarcastic rejoinder that it might sweeten her if she did take sugar.

But he did not make any reference to her unsweet tone, but took the wind out of her sails completely, by saying quietly, 'I remember.'

The next sound she heard was Ellis busy in the kitchen. And she was telling herself then that it meant absolutely nothing that he had remembered from eight years ago that she didn't take sugar. Ellis always had had a memory for detail for goodness sake. And anyway, why was she searching for possible meanings that just hadn't been there in that simple statement, even if he had made it sound as though he had forgotten nothing of that time eight years ago?

And, remembering the utter fool she had made of herself then, Sorrel was fast hoping that his memory might be less than perfect about other matters.

By the time Ellis came back bearing two cups of coffee, there was not a smile in her. As soon as he'd had his coffee, she was going to throw him out—who in the name of thunder did he think he was anyway, calling on her at this time of night?

Having whipped herself up to feeling quite angry with him, Sorrel wasted no time in letting him know that he was backing a loser if he thought he was going to get her to smile again. She waited only until, with a small table between them, he had taken the armchair opposite hers. He looked content to sit there and talk the night away—only did she have news for him!

'How long have you been skulking about out there?' she demanded to know for starters.

The quirk of his mouth, though quickly controlled, told her that her terminology had amused him. 'Round the other corner of your landing, do you mean?' he asked in return, being deliberately obtuse, she knew. The tightening of her mouth told him she was not well pleased with him. But when, instead of giving her the straight answer she was after, he allowed that quirk that had been on his mouth to turn into a mocking smile, and told her, 'Long enough to hear Drury's declaration of love,' Sorrel saw that he was determined to ignore her hostility.

'It didn't occur to you that to eavesdrop on—on what was a very private moment might not be in the best of taste?' she fired.

'You don't think Drury might have been a shade—embarrassed—had I made my presence known while he was down on one knee?' he countered, not rising to the anger coming from her.

Recognising that the heat in the conversation was only one way, Sorrel knew it was the agitation in her to have him there that was making her go off half-cocked. And she was then doing all she could to recapture some cover of sophistication that had been such an enormous help to her on the evening of first seeing him again.

'Perhaps you're right,' she conceded, leaning languidly back in her chair. 'Though I don't suppose for a minute you thought to stick your fingers in your ears.'

The grin he sent her was nearly her undoing. Eight years were wiped away with that grin. She lowered her eyes as she swallowed on a knot of emotion that came and grabbed her by the throat. Ellis used to look like that when she'd trotted out something that tickled his sense of humour. Again she was fighting for control.

But the control she wanted was there when next she looked at him. Though she was grateful that the grin that had stripped those years away had gone. For his face had fallen into stern lines as he looked at her, and his words were telling her that he had not missed seeing her swallow. But she was more than grateful that he had found a different interpretation to put on her emotional moment, when he said:

'You haven't changed, Sorrel—you still hate hurting anyone's feelings, don't you?' Solemnly she looked back, wanting to deny that she hadn't changed, but not quite with him until he added, 'You were remembering that you had to hurt Drury by turning him down, weren't you?'

'It's never pleasant to have to—to hurt someone,' she said quietly.

'No, it isn't,' he agreed, his voice gone gritty, and to her ears, it sounded for all the world as if Ellis too had bled a little that he had once had to hurt her.

Realising then that her imagination had still not learned its lesson from the good hiding Ellis had served it eight years ago, Sorrel firmly killed any thought that he had meant to sound in any way sorry.

'Your coffee's going cold,' she hinted broadly.

She was halfway to downing hers while noting that he was making no move to pick his up, when she very nearly choked on it. For, his voice easy again, no shame in him at his blatant eavesdropping, smoothly he reminded her:

'You told Drury that you didn't want to marry anyone.'

With great difficulty, the sophisticated front she was trying to put across demanding it, Sorrel just managed to control the nerves in her throat that would have seen her choking on her coffee. Ellis Galbraith really was the limit! she thought, and she decided then that she was not going to answer any more of his questions.

He caught the haughty look she sent him that was meant to convey that she would rather have his room than his company. But to her chagrin, he was not the least put out by any look she conjured up in an attempt to try to freeze him.

'Was that remark meant to convey that you never intend to marry?' he went on to ask, entirely oblivious, she thought, that she was no longer seventeen when she had shared her every opinion with him.

Refusing to be drawn, she gave an elegant shrug of her shoulders. With luck he would soon get tired of her non-replies. Then he would go, and she would go to bed—and probably lie there, she thought, and wonder why he had called anyway. Certainly she wasn't going to ask him.

Pointedly she looked at his coffee cup. Then she raised her eyes to his—and warning bells were starting to go off in her head!

She had seen that determined light in his eyes before. Ellis Galbraith had the bit between his teeth. And suddenly, for all he appeared outwardly relaxed, Sorrel knew that Ellis was going nowhere until he had what he had come there for—whatever it was!

'I think you should go,' she said abruptly, not caring to be polite as sudden nerves attacked.

'Were you lying?' he asked, ignoring her trying to turn him out as if she had not spoken. 'Were you lying when you told him,' his eyes were pinning hers as quietly he ended, 'that you were in love with no one?'

Her nerves suddenly froze into a solid block. She was incapable of moving, incapable of saying anything, even if she had any intention of replying. But she almost died when Ellis followed on, still in that same quiet tone, his eyes refusing to let her look away, and said:

'Are you, Sorrel—still in love with me?'

For witless seconds she could do no more than just sit there staring at his stern waiting face. Then, from sheer fright that he should ever know how it was with her, she gave a tinkle of a mocking laugh.

'My God, Ellis,' she scoffed sarcastically, 'have I been *that* obvious!'

She should have known that it would take more than the edge of her tongue to put him off. For he was sticking in there, and to her horror, was determined to wring her dry, as he reminded her:

'You once swore you would always love me.'

'Did I?' she asked, feigning surprise. She emitted another light laugh. 'God, I must have been gauche in those days!'

A fidgeting in her she could not contain made her leave her chair and look pointedly towards the door.

But she had no time for relief to flood in when she saw that Ellis seemed ready now to take the hint. Because as he rose from his chair and moved, again it was not to the door that he moved. And a new light had entered his eyes when, determined not to shy away or let him see her swallow again, she saw he was moving towards her.

'So you're a fully grown woman now,' he said, coming to a stop only when he stood right in front of her.

Not sure what she was supposed to reply to that, Sorrel remained motionless, her eyes watchful. But when one of his hands came up to the side of her face, it was the hardest work to keep up the sophisticated front she was showing. For her heart, never quite steady since he had appeared so unexpectedly, had suddenly started to thunder.

A breathing space came to her when his hand left her cheek. But the 'Goodnight' she had ready on the tip of her tongue, as she suspected his next move would be to go, was never uttered.

For in the next moment, in a smooth though lightning movement, both his hands were in her hair, and before she knew it, the pins that confined her elegant chignon were dropping unheeded to the carpet anywhere they fell. And as her hair tumbled down about her shoulders, so too fell her only protection— her look of sophistication.

'Now you look more like the girl I once knew,' breathed Ellis, a look of satisfaction in his eyes as he surveyed the change his handiwork had performed.

'You can just jolly well ...' she tried as, panic-stricken, she saw a warm look come to his eyes. She never got to finish—for suddenly Ellis had taken her in his arms.

She had felt panic-stricken before, but with his arms around her, Sorrel felt near to fainting. She wanted to remain cool, calm, and collected. But for years she had been starved of his touch.

She pushed at him as she tried to listen to her head, but the battle she was trying to put up was lost without a fight when, refusing to let her go, Ellis brought his mouth down over hers.

An inner sigh went up in her as bliss filled her soul. Ease from the pain that was in her was there as, held close against his heart, Ellis's mouth gentle on hers, she clung to him as if he was some life support she could not do without.

She was not conscious that her arms had gone up and around him. She was unaware that as each kiss became warmer and deeper, she was responding fully and with every fibre of her being. All she knew was that there had been an aching need in her for his touch, his kiss, and that with her heart for once ruling her head, she could no longer deny that aching need.

'Lovely Sorrel,' murmured Ellis, when his mouth left hers, his fingers pushing the shoulder-straps of her dress down her arms as he kissed and caressed the satin smoothness of her skin. 'I want you so much,' he breathed, a thickness in his voice thrilling her that she had this effect on him.

Again he kissed her mouth, passion mounting between them, so that when she was prevented by the shoulder-straps of her dress being down around her arms from putting her arms around him, when Ellis with a warm questioning look at her went to unzip the back of her dress, she had not the smallest objection to make.

Glad to be rid of the confining garment, as her dress

slipped to the floor she stepped away from the garment, and Ellis threw off his jacket.

She saw his eyes go down to the flimsy covering of her lacy bra, but she had no time to feel in any way shy. For a groan left him and he picked her up in his arms, his head coming down, his mouth finding hers and staying over her lips as he carried her into the bedroom.

To lie with him, to feel him this close on her bed, to know that he wanted her with the same passion that she wanted him, was the extent of Sorrel's thinking in that heady moment of having Ellis pressing his body yet closer to hers.

'My lovely darling,' he breathed, to send her into seventh heaven, his hands caressing her, taking her on an upward heady spiral.

She was barely aware that expert fingers had found the clip to release her bra, but she was still not holding back as she heard his passionate murmur, the wonder in him as his eyes left her flushed face, and he feasted his eyes on the creamy globes of her naked breasts.

'How beautiful you are,' he whispered, and there was no thought in Sorrel of turning back when warm hands caressed her breasts, the pink hardening tips beneath his touch delighting him so that he just had to kiss each crimsoned pinnacle in turn, his lips straying down past her waist to kiss the curve of her belly.

Sorrel was in a heaven of rapture when he allowed her to help him out of his shirt, her fingers moving freely on his bare chest. Her whole body was tingling at the feel of the rough hair the moment before her breasts were crushed by that same chest as his body came over hers.

As she had helped him off with his shirt, when some

minutes had passed and her need for him had her
moaning out that need, she helped Ellis remove the rest
of her clothes. Shyness only overcame her when, as she
lay naked by him, he pulled back so that he could see
the length of her unclad body.

Quickly then she moved to kiss him, and her rapture
was near to being complete when he told her, 'You're
so beautiful, my darling. You're body is perfection. Is it
any wonder I couldn't keep away?'

'You—wanted to keep away?' she whispered, and
had his mouth on hers again the moment he had
breathed:

'I tried hard—but I couldn't keep away from you any
longer.'

A symphony cascading in her ears to hear his
confession, Sorrel was almost beside herself with
wanting him. Again he kissed her, his hands stroking
down her naked back, her shapely bottom and her
thighs. Her heart was hammering like no other
hammering she had ever felt when his hands came to
her waist and he pulled her close and kissed her, and
then sent her into ecstasy when he groaned:

'You've got to be mine, Sorrel. I must have you living
with me.'

'Oh, Ellis!' she moaned, and was not sure then that
she was not going to cry.

A second later she very nearly did begin to weep. But
not from any happiness that, surely, Ellis had been
asking her to marry him and go to live with him in his
home in Kent.

For, his ardour still ruling him, at her sounding
delighted to be his, Ellis kissed her again, crushing her
slender body in his arms as he murmured, 'I can't take
the thought of some other man paying your bills.'

Cold shock hit her then. Though for a few stunned seconds she lay passive in his arms. But when ice-cold horror struck hard that somehow she was lying stark naked in the arms of a man who she had once given the power to bitterly wound her, so she was leaping from the bed and with shaking hands was snatching up a robe and wrapping it hurriedly about her. The knowledge was hammering at her then that should she take up Ellis's offer of marriage, since she would have to confess how she came by her money, there was just no way she could trust him not to spurn her as once before he had spurned her—though this time it would be with destroying contempt.

A flicked glance at him showed his face was a picture of amazement that only a moment ago she had been nestling up to him moaning for more. But his amazement was to change to stupefied astonishment, when, finding what she could in the way of a voice, coldly Sorrel told him:

'I believe I told you, s-some time back, that you'd outstayed your welcome.' She turned from his astonishment as she told him, 'I'd be glad if you would kindly leave.'

'Leave!'

Just the one word left him. But the next moment he was off the bed, and she was feeling his hands rough on her shoulders and was having to face dark angry smouldering eyes as he spun her round to face him. There was nothing of the lover he had been then when harshly he gritted:

'What the hell's just got into you?'

Never more did Sorrel need to disguise her true self. But with her hair flowing down about her shoulders, her loose-fitting robe bearing no resemblance to the ultra-smart dress she had raised no objection to him removing from her, she did what she could to gather round her an air of cool detached sophistication.

'Really, Ellis,' she drawled, determined not to wince as his fingers bit into her shoulders, 'did I create such a fuss that morning you threw me out in the middle of a—passionate—interlude?'

He reeled back as though she had just struck him, instant recall his, as on a stunned breath, he exclaimed, 'My God!' his look incredulous as he charged, 'You're trying to tell me that your response to me just now was faked, put on—because you wanted to get even for something that happened—eight years ago!'

His astonishment had been mammoth before, but his shaken look made Sorrel very nearly cave in and confess the whole of it, telling him what had only just occurred to her.

But she had learned a hard lesson once, and as a glint came to Ellis's eyes that she was not backing down from her statement, which meant that she must be a hard case to have kept her head while pretending otherwise, all her instincts of self-preservation came out in full force.

'It's been quite a night, Ellis,' she drawled, observing the glint in his eyes had turned to ice at her aloof air, the furious way he jerked into his shirt telling her he would be making no attempt to persuade her back to that bed. 'But two proposals in one night are enough for any girl.' A thought suddenly struck her. 'Or was your proposal more in the way of a proposition?'

Ellis looked at her only once before, furious, he strode from her apartment. But that one look was so enraged that only then did she guess that it was leave— or give her something to remember him by—as scathingly he tossed at her:

'Either way, proposal or proposition, I've more than enough to keep you in the style to which you've *become* accustomed!'

One way or another, Sorrel thought, still sitting where she had collapsed an hour earlier, it had been an emotional evening. First there had been that upset with Cynthia Armitage. Then she had been upset that she had had to hurt Rod. And now this latest upset that put both other emotional upsets well into the shade.

She wished that she could cry—but she could not. She felt defeated, dead inside—and never had she felt more unhappy.

CHAPTER FIVE

FIRMLY deciding that she had thought enough about Ellis Galbraith and was not going to waste another second on going over again all that had kept her sleepless, Sorrel left her bed the next morning and, needing action, set herself to cleaning her flat straight away.

But, as if everything was determined to conspire against her fixing her mind on anything but him, the hairpins she had to bend to pick up from her living room carpet soon brought Ellis back with her. To remember that she had put up no sort of a fight when he had removed those pins from her hair and had taken her in his arms, brought the tears she had not shed last night very near to the surface.

'Damn him,' she whispered, but there was no hate in the sound. And Ellis was there in her head for the rest of the day. She had known deep down that it wouldn't be easy to keep him out.

Though there was no doubt in her mind that day that Ellis's suggestion that she go and live with him had not been the proposal she, with her senses all out of gear, had last night been crazy enough to think it had been. Oh, he had desired her, there had been no mistaking that. And he had been as mad as fury when, thank the lord, from somewhere the notion had come to her to tell him that she had just been playing at evening up old scores.

For a moment her heart fluttered in panic as she

wondered if she had given away too much of herself. Her response, she vividly recalled, had been all that any man could ask. But, she thought, wasn't that so much the better? She had wanted Ellis to believe her a hard case, and no longer affected by him. What better way to get him to believe that she had changed from the softhearted girl she had once been into a cool, calculating hard nut of a woman? By her cheating him at the last minute the way she had, surely by now there must be no doubt in his mind that the Sorrel Maitland he once knew no longer existed.

The memory of how she had been with him, how Ellis had been with her, was still catching her out the next day. But it was on the following day that she was able to decide just why it was he had told her, 'I can't take the thought of some other man paying your bills'. Ellis had a possessive streak she had not known about.

Had she gone to live with him for a month or so, or however long the dalliance would have lasted, he would want to possess her wholly for that period of time. He had merely been stating the fact that living with him meant that he wanted sole rights, and would insist that he be the only one to provide everything she required.

What more proof did she want? He had cut Wenda Sykes out of his heart, out of his life, when, while she was engaged to him, he had discovered that she was taking everything he couldn't give her financially from another man.

Her telephone had been remarkably quiet of late, but when it started ringing on Thursday, Sorrel's heart went instantly erratic. That was until common sense told her she would be lucky if Ellis so much as afforded her the curt nod he had given Wenda should they ever bump into each other again.

Secure in the knowledge that Ellis's fingers would never again dial her number, Sorrel picked up the phone and, with a sense of surprise heard, contrary to her expectations, that it was Rod Drury who had dialled her number.

'Hello, Rod,' she greeted him evenly, what little thoughts she had had to spare for him sad for the hurt she had caused him. But she had not been too upset that she would not be going out with him again.

The preliminaries of how was she, and wasn't the weather nice, out of the way, Sorrel felt immediate inner agitation stir when Rod went on to remind her that it was his parents' wedding anniversary tomorrow.

'I—have remembered,' she replied slowly, hoping with all her heart that what it sounded as though she might hear him say next was not going to be what he would say—though say it he did.

'You're still coming with me?' he asked.

'I don't think that's a very good idea, Rod,' she replied as gently as she could.

'Because I rushed you by asking you to marry me?'

'I ...' She hesitated. She did not want to hurt him again, but as she saw it then, hearing a suggestion in his tone that he might at some later date again ask her to marry him, there was nothing for it but to be blunt. 'Yes,' she agreed. 'But it wouldn't have done any good had you waited. I just don't want to be married.'

'I see,' he replied, and she thought then that he would soon be saying goodbye. But to her consternation, he was returning to the subject of his parents' wedding anniversary, and telling her, 'I'd like my parents to be happy this weekend, Sorrel.'

'I'm sure they will be,' she said, remembering she had

thought before that Moira and Neville Drury had one of the few good marriages around.

'The thing is,' Rod persisted, delaying that goodbye, 'my parents do have a sort of blind spot where I'm concerned.'

'Oh?' said Sorrel warily.

'Mm,' he murmured. 'They know me so well, and if I go down by myself they're sure to think that we've had a row, and that I'm in the doldrums—it's bound to put a blight on what should be a perfect weekend for them.'

'You've taken other girls home before,' she said quickly, her instinct to be wary not playing her false, she saw. 'Why not call up one of your other . . .'

'My parents invited you,' Rod pointed out when she would rather that he hadn't. 'And besides,' he added, 'quite honestly, you're the only girl I want at my home this weekend.' And, not allowing her to get a word in, 'Also it wouldn't be fair all round, on my parents,' he put in to give another weakening prod to her resolve, 'or any girl I took home, whom I didn't want to take.'

'I'm sure you're . . .' Sorrel didn't get to add 'exaggerating the case' before he was butting in:

'I promise I won't propose again, if that's what's bothering you,' further promising, as he urged, 'Come with me, Sorrel. We'll just be good pals this weekend, nothing more. I'll give you my word on that. It would mean so much to the parents.'

Sorrel put down the phone, already regretting that she had given in and said she would go. Had Rod given her a minute to breathe instead of rushing on and on to play on her conscience, to finally pressgang her by reminding her that by accepting their invitation she had as good as promised his parents that she would be there, then she was sure she could have found some good counter-argument.

The problem was that, not expecting his phone call, indeed, not expecting to hear from him again, she had had no excuse ready. And the last thing she could have told him was the only excuse that had been in the forefront of her mind the whole time—that she didn't want to go because she was afraid that Ellis Galbraith might be there.

It was while she was putting into a case all she thought she would need for the weekend that mutiny suddenly asserted itself. Why should she be afraid of meeting Ellis again, for heaven's sake? she questioned angrily. She owed him nothing, just as, after the last time she had met him, he owed her nothing. And anyway, hadn't she already come to the conclusion that should they ever bump into each other again then there would be no conversation between them? She closed the lid of her case with a snap—he wasn't even going to give a nod in her direction, was he?

True to his word, when Rod Drury came to call for her on Friday afternoon, his demeanour was that of a good friend. There was nothing in his manner to make her feel uncomfortable as he steered his car away from her apartment block. And by the time he had turned into the drive of his parents' home, Sorrel was growing of the opinion that but for the party that was to be held that night, she might well enjoy this weekend more than she had thought.

'I've given you the same room you had last time,' said Moira with a smile once their greetings were out of the way, going on to tell her, 'My two sisters and their husbands are here for the weekend too, and also Neville's brother and his wife. They're all horse-mad, of course, and are round at the stables at the moment. But we'll be having tea presently, then you'll be able to meet them all.'

'Meantime,' put in Rod, 'I'll take Sorrel's case up to her room. I've got to go up to change anyway,' he said, having called for her straight from his office. But he did not try to linger outside the door of her room, and his casual, 'See you in about fifteen minutes,' as they went their separate ways, was a further endorsement for her that Rod was putting aside his own feelings for the sake of keeping this weekend a happy one for his parents.

Liking him more than she had ever done because of it, Sorrel did her small unpacking. She rinsed her hands and repaired her light make-up, and then, thinking that a cup of tea wouldn't be a bad idea, she left her room. She met Rod coming away from his door and went with him down the stairs to an ante-room, which was doing fill-in service since the carpet in the drawing room had been taken up in preparation for dancing later.

A lively sound of conversation greeted them when they went in. But Sorrel soon saw what a nice family Rod had, as in turn she shook hands with aunts and uncles and a couple of cousins.

Over tea-cups, horses inevitably coming into the conversation from time to time, Sorrel learned that there was to be a family dinner early that evening, but that later it would be open house with all and sundry invited. But if her thoughts would have strayed to thoughts of Ellis being there too, then as the talk again returned to horses, she pushed Ellis out of her mind and concentrated her attention on what was being said.

By the sound of it, Moira and Neville and all the relations were going to enjoy a day in the saddle tomorrow. Lunch, she heard, had already been organised at the *Pig and Flute* out Habberleigh way, wherever Habberleigh was.

She was starting to feel enthusiastic herself, although

she did not ride and would not be part of the happy
band setting out in the morning, when Rod suddenly
said, 'If the weather stays like this, you'll have a terrific
day,' and a hush descended on the room as everyone
looked at him. There was disbelief in one of his aunt's
tones when, looking scandalised, she asked:

'You're surely not suggesting that you aren't coming
with us, Roderick?'

Since he was every day of twenty-nine, Rod's grin
broke free to have his aunt speak to him as if he were
ten years old. ''Fraid so, Aunt,' he replied cheerfully.

'But . . .' his aunt started to protest.

'Sorrel doesn't ride, Sybil,' said Moira swiftly, with a
friendly smile at Sorrel. 'So naturally Rod . . .'

'Doesn't ride . . .?' echoed Sybil faintly, making
Sorrel want to giggle when it appeared she had
committed a cardinal sin. Though her feeling of
wanting to giggle quickly departed when that good lady
recovered, and promptly turned to her brother to state,
'Well surely, Neville, if you haven't got one, you can
borrow some sort of a hack from somewhere which the
young lady can sit on without coming to grief. We don't
want to split the party up.'

'The party isn't going to be split up,' Sorrel got in
quickly, the idea of bumping over field and meadow
like a sack of potatoes, with her holding everyone up
when they wanted to gallop off, having not the slightest
appeal. 'Rod was only joking about not coming with
you, weren't you, Rod?'

She hoped he read in her eyes what she was trying to
convey without her actually having to say it—that the
good pals they were supposed to be this weekend meant
that he did not have to keep constantly by her side for
the whole of that time.

For serious moments Rod looked back at her. Then, with a teasing look at his aunt, he remarked generally, 'Anything to get Aunt Sybil going.' But under cover of much laughter, he turned his attention to Sorrel, to say, 'We do have a sedate horse in the stables if you'd like . . .'

'Actually, I'd rather set my mind on taking myself off for a good long hike,' she invented quickly. Blisters on her heels, in her view, were far preferable to not being able to sit down for a week. Though in truth, she rather enjoyed walking.

Dinner that night was about the merriest dinner party Sorrel had ever attended. Neville Drury made a delightful little speech about the joy he had known thirty years ago when Moira had become his wife, and the joy that had been his ever since.

Touched by the way he had spoken, by the way he looked at Moira and Moira had looked back at him, as champagne corks popped, Sorrel was having an uphill battle to remember that sophisticated girls did not cry at sentimental moments.

Once dinner was over, everyone moved to the gaily decorated drawing room to await the arrival of other guests. The time Sorrel had not been looking forward to was there.

Though when the dancing had been under way for about an hour, and with no sign of Ellis putting in an appearance, she began to relax. That the evening had lost some of its sparkle because she was not going to have a glimpse of his dark good looks was preferable, she thought, to the ache she would have to hide had he been there and, as she knew would happen, he cut her dead.

Not lacking for partners, she was just about to refuse

the invitation of one earnest young man to take the floor again, when, her eyes flicking to the door as they had done surreptitiously for most of the evening, her heart missed a beat, then hurried up with more speed than was necessary to catch up on that missed beat.

'I'd love to,' she replied to the young man waiting to take her in his arms.

She smiled up at him as they danced by the door, her eyes fixed on his face lest her inner self betrayed her and her eyes strayed.

Fortunately, when the dance came to an end and it looked as if she was going to have some difficulty in shaking off her ambitious partner, Rod was there to rescue her.

'Enjoying yourself?' he enquired, his hold on her nothing she could object to as, an excellent dancer, he whisked her round the floor.

Despite herself, her eyes went to the door. Ellis was not there. She turned her head, her eyes searching. A sick jealousy invaded her when she saw that the man her eyes were looking for had eyes for no one but the utterly ravishing blonde he had in his arms, as he too circuited the floor.

'Er—fantastic,' she replied, rather belatedly as, collecting herself, she realised that Rod was waiting for an answer to his question.

'You're not regretting that you came?'

Again she caught a glimpse of a dark head that to her mind was much too close to a blonde one. 'No,' she lied valiantly, never in her life having felt such an emotion as the one that had taken charge of her, and would have had her leaving Rod and going to pull that blonde away from Ellis's arms—had she been unable to control it.

'You're sure you don't mind about me going riding tomorrow?' asked Rod, while Sorrel was in the depths of remembering that not a week ago, those same arms that now encircled the blonde had been round her own naked body.

'I'd mind if you didn't,' she said, and pulled herself firmly together. She was determined then not to care who Ellis danced with—though she could be sure that he wouldn't be coming over to ask her for a dance.

By the time Ellis had danced twice more with the blonde, once with another equally stunning-looking girl, and then once again with the blonde, Sorrel, ready to call it a night and go to her bed, was certain that she wouldn't dance with him even if he did ask her.

She too had rarely been off the dancing area, but determinedly, not looking for a snub, she had avoided any chance of eye contact with Ellis; not that he even knew she was there.

But it was when she had got to the point of wondering if she was expected to stay down until the last of the guests other than family had gone that she discovered that Ellis did know she was there. She was concentrating on not looking over to where she had last seen him, while waiting for someone who had introduced himself as Graeme to return with the thirst-quencher he had gone for, when she looked up, her heart starting to race even as she made every effort to appear cool, to find that Ellis had come to stand by her.

For ageless moments, as his eyes took in the controlled look of her in her flame-coloured dress with its delicate shoulder-straps, as she had expected, he did not have one word to say to her. Then, to her surprise, far from cutting her dead, 'Are you going to dance with me, Sorrel Maitland?' he asked, and there was a challenge there in his voice, just as though he suspected she was afraid to go into his arms.

Which had to be odd, she thought, since she had shown him most plainly how easily she could turn away from those arms. But, about to accept his invitation, to show him again how little having his arms about her could leave her affected, she felt jealousy choose that moment to take a swipe at her as the thought came that he was only asking her to dance with him because the blonde had gone to powder her nose.

'Some other time, perhaps,' she murmured coolly. 'Graeme will be here with my drink in a moment.'

The slight narrowing of his eyes told her that Ellis did not care very much for her cool arrogance. But her arrogance was left floundering when, to her sudden astonishment, Sorrel found that tonight Ellis Galbraith was not in a mind to take no for an answer.

'Let Graeme drink it,' he said, and smoothly, taking her off guard, he had reached for her, and had her feet moving in step with his, the choice of whether she wanted to dance with him or no taken from her.

A spurt of anger surfaced as she got over her astonishment. But she was mindful that any eyes interested enough to be watching her footwork might be surprised at the new sort of vicious step if she aimed the kick he warranted at his shin. Sorrel controlled her ire and managed to keep all expression from her face.

They had danced round the room a couple of times, when, his first comment since he had waltzed her on to the floor, Ellis said:

'I didn't expect to see you here tonight.'

Ignoring the fact that by now her heart was trying to escape through her ribs, she guessed he meant that in the circumstances of the way they had parted, he had thought she would prefer not to risk bumping into him again. Aware that he was waiting for her to answer something to his statement, almost she did not reply. But as far as he was to know, she had been as cool then, as she had shot from the bed, as she was trying to appear now.

'Oh,' she drawled, as if she had no memory of that occasion, 'why, I wonder?'

'Isn't it obvious?' he answered—but was successful in making her affected airy manner abruptly depart, when he revealed that his thoughts had been along totally different lines from her own, as he added, 'Since you'd turned Drury down, I would have thought it kinder not to have seen him again.'

'I'd accepted the invitation ages ago,' Sorrel said quickly in her defence. 'Rod wanted me . . .' she broke off, all too well aware that by attempting to defend herself she had lost some of her poise. The dance music ended, and she pulled out of his arms, once more in possession of herself now that Ellis was not touching her. 'Anyhow,' she resumed, lofty now, no intention in her then of explaining herself to him, 'who told you I was kind?'

She would have walked away from him without another word then. But before she could complete more than one step, her arm was taken in a firm grip, and she found she was facing the open French doors as she heard Ellis, a smile for anyone who was watching on his face, say pleasantly:

'It is warm in here, isn't it?' every bit as though she had just complained of feeling overheated. The next thing she knew, she was outside the house with him, his hand still firm on her arm, as he walked her across the lawn.

As Sorrel saw it then, she had two choices. Either she gave him the sharp edge of her tongue and, since he didn't look to be ready to let go his hold on her arm, have an undignified struggle to be free of him. Or she could play it cool.

'It's a lovely night, isn't it?' she remarked—coolness had been her ally before.

His hold on her arm relaxed. But he still was not playing the game according to the rules. For he was not letting go of the subject that had begun at the end of the dance, she heard as, ignoring her pleasantry, he picked up the conversation where she had left it with her question of who had told him she was kind.

'You always were kind, Sorrel,' he resumed. 'There wasn't a stray cat that came into the workshop that didn't get fed.'

'So I like animals,' she shrugged.

'Cats, dogs, children, old ladies,' he went on, 'you were kind to everyone.'

As she thought she was glad he had not mentioned her kindness to old men, a shiver went through her. Her shiver must have communicated itself to him, though not the cause—her fear of his killing contempt if he ever found out about her kindness, and its reward certainly most definitely unlooked for, a reward nevertheless for her affection and kindness to one old gentleman.

'You're cold,' said Ellis. But instead of turning her about and taking her indoors as she had thought the most likely solution, he continued to stroll with her, his hand leaving her arm to come about her shoulders in what she supposed was his way of keeping her warm.

'It's—remarkable how people change, isn't it?' she remarked, her insides not belonging to her, to the trite person she was trying to be as she realised that she did not want to go indoors; but that she must. Already they were some way from the house—not that Ellis was likely to try anything after that last episode, the way he had his arm around her was completely unsexual, she thought.

'I'll agree we all move on,' he replied, his voice even, unhurried. 'But we all keep those same intrinsic qualities that shaped us. Basically,' he went on conversationally, 'I believe we all stay the same.'

Whether he knew it or not, his voice was starting to seduce her, and Sorrel wasn't having that. 'Study philosophy, did you?' she asked smartly. But she could have saved her breath. For she hadn't rattled him, she saw, and his tone still had that seductive power to it, as he continued.

'In fact, I thought you had stayed the girl who was always kind to children, when I had reason to return to the Kinglingham area some years ago.'

'You returned to Kinglingham?' she exclaimed, without realising it coming to a halt, not moving as she thought that 'some years ago' she had still been in the area, that they might have been walking along adjacent streets, and she had never known it.

Ellis had come to a halt too, his arm falling from her shoulders. 'As a matter of fact, I thought I spotted you with a couple of children,' he said quietly, his expression hidden in the darkness. 'I almost came over and said "Hello",' he went on when Sorrel was starting to wonder, had it been her he had seen? It could have been. Cynthia Armitage's unmotherly attitude of wanting 'those squalling brats' where she couldn't see or hear them had meant that they had spent a lot of time out of the house.

'But it wasn't me?' she asked, wondering now, that

hard shell she had grown not so hard about her then, what she would have done if Ellis had come up to her in the street and said a casual 'Hello'.

Ellis, she thought, was a long time answering her question. But, 'How could it have been?' he replied at last. 'You've never been married, have you?'

That didn't stop her being fully capable of looking after other people's children, she thought. Though she knew that it hadn't been her he had seen but someone who must look like her. For there was nothing wrong with his eyesight or his memory, and he had seen her almost every day when she had worked for him—he had recognised her eight years on without difficulty.

'No,' she replied, 'I've never married.'

'And,' he went on, pausing to ask lightly, 'excuse the question, nor have you ever had children, have you, Sorrel?'

'Question excused,' she replied equally lightly. 'No, I've never had any children.' Suddenly she was feeling most irrationally disappointed that she had missed seeing him when he had been in the Kinglingham area, for she would probably have flushed scarlet and stammered all over the place had she been taken out of her stride in those days, by meeting him unexpectedly. It was about time, she then thought, that they returned to the house.

She did in fact attempt to turn around and start walking back the way they had come. But, as before, suddenly Ellis's firm hold was on her arm, and he was staying her from going anywhere. And she was having to wrestle with not only what just the feel of his touch could do to her, but the panicky thudding of her heart that resulted from his saying softly all at once:

'Why have you never married, Sorrel?'

She tried one of her airy shrugs. But she was suddenly tense, and it didn't come off. The sharp acid words she wanted just would not come—and were still in hiding when Ellis, not waiting for her to reply, went on to positively stun her that he *must* have been asking her to marry him when he had asked her to go and live with him, for he said:

'You left me in no doubt the other night that you didn't fancy marriage with me as your husband, but . . .'

'You were *serious*?' shot from her, not an atom of sham about her then. 'You were asking me to marry you when . . .' She broke off. She was still trying to get herself together when, mockingly she thought, he drawled:

'I did get a little—hot under the collar, didn't I?' And again not waiting for her reply as, with the recollection as vivid as ever in her mind, Sorrel was recalling that he had been not only collarless at the time, but shirtless too, he said, 'But then you're a heady woman, Sorrel— you were at seventeen.' And while she was thinking that this was the first she'd heard that she had been heady to him at seventeen, he was saying, 'Though since you're not going to hold me to anything I said in a—rash— moment, let's say that we both had a lucky escape.'

'I'll second that,' said Sorrel, with as much sophistication as she could muster, which in truth, she had to own, was not much.

'Good,' he said. 'Now answer my question.'

'I've forgotten what it was,' she lied, and made another attempt to go back the way they had come. But his hold on her arm was as firm as ever, with no objection in him whatsoever to refreshing her memory.

'I asked you why it was you had never married,' he repeated his question.

She attempted another shrug of her shoulders—
wasted, she thought in the darkness, since Ellis could
not see much more than her outline. Though for all he
might have felt her uncaring movement, he was still
determined not to let go of her until she had answered.

'I suppose I—just never fancied anyone enough,' she
said, the best she could do in the way of an answer,
since he appeared to know that it was not from lack of
chances that she had remained single.

'Never fancied anyone enough,' he murmured. But
his voice was serious, all mockery departed, when
quietly he dropped out, 'Or never trusted anyone
enough, Sorrel?'

The jerk of her muscle as he hit on the rest of it was
something she could do nothing about. But her voice
had gone hard, when she told him shortly:

'Trust is for kids.'

Regardless of the indignity of it then, she pulled her
arm from his hold. But she didn't get to walk more than
two paces from him, before he was after her. Both his
arms came around her then, and he was pulling her
head against his chest, his voice gentle, regretful even,
as softly he asked:

'Did I do this to you?' And, his voice thickening,
'Was it me, Sorrel, who made you so that you won't let
anyone get close to you?'

Having to accept that he wasn't going to let her free
was one thing. But she was not going to let him make
her suffer ever again, not if she could help it.

'My God!' she raised her head to scorn. She would
have trotted out her well-worn phrase about his conceit
then—had he given her the chance.

But he did not give her the chance. For as though he
would salve all the hurt in her he had ever inflicted,

tenderly Ellis held her to him. Gently his mouth came over hers, and his kiss was all giving. And Sorrel wanted to cry at the beauty of his kiss that might have been healing, if she could only let it be.

But Ellis had hurt her once most traumatically. She had not wanted to fall in love with him—and he could hurt her again. His arms around her were now a caress, no more. Sorrel found she did not need all her strength to push him away. And push him away she did, his tender kiss having to be broken before he broke her.

'You're mistaken, Ellis, if you think that no man has ever got close to me,' she said, her tones like ice because they had to be.

She heard his sharp intake of breath, and knew she was reaching him when, his voice as cold as hers, he asked, 'You're saying that some man since me . . .'

Her tinkling laugh cut him off. 'That's what I'm saying.' Mockery was hers now.

'Who?' to her astonishment he was demanding to know.

But she was ready with an answer, her astonishment stemming from nothing more than that he should have the nerve to demand who, besides himself, she had been close to.

'Who else,' she asked lightly, 'but the man who pays for my flat, my car, my clothes . . .'

She remembered Ellis had said, in a heated moment, admittedly, that he could not bear the thought of any man paying her bills. She guessed he was heated again. For his voice was little short of savage when, still demanding to be answered, he snarled the question:

'You love him—this man?'

She had been very fond of old Mr Ollerenshaw—she

didn't think he would mind. 'Dearly,' she tossed at him.

When Sorrel started to walk, she found that Ellis was no longer in any mind to try and detain her. Her head high, she kept on walking until she reached the house.

CHAPTER SIX

THERE were a few sore heads around the breakfast table the following morning, but nothing Sybil proclaimed, that a good gallop would not cure. One and all agreed that it had been a super party.

'Are you sure you won't come with us?' asked Rod beneath the hum of the general conversation going on. 'I can soon find you a mount. And I promise not to go off and leave you to cope on your own,' he tried to persuade.

Sorrel shook her head, even as she was thinking what a likeable, considerate person he was. Not only was she averse to spoiling his fun by having to rein in his own horse to wait for her all the while, but neither did she want any special attentions from him.

'I've set my heart on a walk,' she smiled.

'Well, why not have your walk, then come over to Habberleigh and join us for lunch? You can take my car,' he said, and would have warmed to his theme. But again she was shaking her head.

'It's ages since I took a really long walk,' she told him, and smiled again as Moira Drury looked her way. 'I've no idea where I might be come lunchtime.'

'There's some lovely scenery around here,' joined in Rod's mother. 'But if you intend to be out that long, I'll get Mrs Richards to prepare you a packed lunch.'

Not wanting to put anyone to any trouble—in Sorrel's view the staff had more than enough to do in putting the house to rights after last night's festivities without

the extra work having a houseful of guests involved—
she shook her head. But Moira would not listen to any
protest, and when breakfast was over and people
charged in all directions getting hard riding hats and
anything else they needed, Moira went to consult with
her housekeeper and Sorrel returned to her room.

Having not thought when she had packed that she
would be exploring the countryside on foot, she saw
that her smart linen trouser suit would have to do
stand duty for the jeans and shirt she would have
preferred for her ramble. Though, thank goodness, she
had thought to put in a pair of flat-heeled shoes.

Rod was in the hall when she went downstairs again,
and she went with him to the stables where, amid the
sound of horses hooves and much jocularity, everyone
moved off. Rod was the last to go, his smile trying to
cover the wistful look in his eyes as he said:

'I wish you were coming, Sorrel. But enjoy your walk.'

'Enjoy your ride,' she returned, and as he and his
horse started to move off, she went back to the house.

Had Mrs Richards had her way, Sorrel would have
set off for her walk with a fair-sized picnic basket in her
hands. But, her lunch reduced to a manageable parcel
of sandwiches with an outer covering of plastic because,
according to Mrs Richards, 'It's going to rain,' she
eventually left the house.

For all the sun was refusing to shine, to her eyes it
didn't look as though it was going to rain. But
conceding that the housekeeper might well have a
weather corn, within a very few minutes the weather
was the last thing on Sorrel's mind.

She hadn't seen Ellis again after she had told him
that she dearly loved the benefactor of her flat, and
everything else, and had walked from him. So whether

he had cut across the lawn and walked home, or if he'd had to go to his car and had driven home, she had no way of knowing.

Having taken a country path, when Sorrel spotted a house a short way up ahead, her footsteps halted. She had no idea if that house was Ellis's or if it wasn't. What she did know was that his house was in the near vicinity and that she had no wish to see him again. Within the next ten yards she had taken a sharp right turn—the house at the back of her was soon getting further and further away.

Of course it was more than likely, her thoughts picked up her temporarily dropped subject, that Ellis had made some arrangement to meet that blonde who'd been hanging on to his every word the last time she had seen them dancing together. For she had been nowhere to be seen either when she'd made it back to the drawing room.

It annoyed Sorrel that she should feel a dart of pain that Ellis might have kissed the blonde in that same beautiful way he had kissed her out there in the garden. Oh, damn him, she thought, a dry sob catching her out.

For the next hour she trudged on, purposefully ejecting Ellis Galbraith from her mind whenever he tried to take over her thoughts.

Discovering that she had been hurrying when she had all day for her walk and nothing to hurry over, Sorrel came to a stile, and finding she was quite hot, although the sky had now turned to a threatening grey, she took off her jacket and rested a while.

When a few drops of rain fell to dampen her shirt, she found them welcome. She donned her jacket again only when her body heat had dropped. Her small parcel was starting to become an encumbrance, and for a moment or two she toyed with the idea of getting rid of it. The wildlife she thought, would soon demolish her sandwiches.

Conscience pricking when she thought of Mrs Richards leaving what she was doing in what was sure to be a very busy day, to prepare the sandwiches, prevented her. That, plus the fact that not having her handbag with her or so much as a pocket in her jacket, she would have to carry her litter home with her anyway.

Sorrel left the stile and for another half an hour she walked on. As Moira Drury had said, there were some beautiful views in this part of the world. But as rain started to fall again, thunder rumbling ominously in the distance, she was beginning to think she had better start looking for some kind of shelter.

Shelter was at hand, she saw, when, as the heavens opened, she rounded a clump of trees. For, in view of the thunder rejecting to shelter in the trees, Sorrel saw not far away, in splendid isolation, a substantial looking house where she was sure that no one would mind if she stood under the eaves until this downpour was over.

She was halfway between the house and the trees, the rain now coming down like hurtling stair-rods, when the thought she had had before, that Ellis had his home somewhere around here, stopped her dead.

She was oblivious to the fact that the rain had taken on monsoon proportions and that her elegant suit was being soaked. Trepidation had her in its grip. She always felt like just so much jelly after contact with Ellis. Suppose it was his house? Suppose he was at home? Suppose . . .

She stopped supposing when through rain-soaked eyelashes she saw the tall figure of a man coming from the house. That he was mindless of the torrents soaking his trousers and sweater was made plain when he began walking unhurriedly towards her.

Recognising Ellis immediately, Sorrel was ready to run away—but pride came to halt her movement before she could take off. Already Ellis had suggested that she was not able to trust any man, and he was the cause. Thanks to Mr Ollerenshaw she had been able to put him right about her not letting any man get close to her since Ellis had parted company with her. But what would he think now if the moment he approached she took to her heels and bolted like some startled colt?

She had left it too late to run anyway, she saw, for with his hair plastered wetly to his head—so lord knew what hers looked like—Ellis had already reached her. His face wore an inscrutable expression. No sign there of his being out of sorts with her or anything else that she could see, as, conversationally ignoring the fact that by now he was as soaked as she was, he commented laconically:

'Out for a stroll?'

Why that comment should amuse her, she couldn't think. He must have known that she had walked miles, but perhaps it did seem rather ridiculous to be engaged in what appeared to be a normal conversation when they were both becoming more and more saturated by the second.

Without a smile, she answered, 'Everybody's gone riding for the day,' which sounded inane, even to her own ears. 'I thought I'd have a picnic,' she added, which sounded even more inane in view of the downpour, she thought, as she indicated the parcel in her hand.

Ellis taking the parcel from her one hand, and taking hold of her other hand with one of his, set her heart bumping as he started to lead her to the house.

'Where are we going?' she asked, and wondered then, since it was obvious where they were going, if the rain had dampened her normally brighter wits.

'Standing about in all this sun isn't good for you,' said Ellis, his face deliberately solemn, she felt. And indicating the Georgian building in front of them, he added evenly, 'This is my house.'

All sense of being amused rapidly left Sorrel. The appalling thought suddenly occurred to her that Ellis thought she had known where he lived when she had set out on her walk. That . . .

'I wasn't coming to see you,' she blurted as they reached the gate he had left open.

He favoured her with a tight-lipped look. 'I know *that*,' he told her tersely, and pushed her in front of him through the gateway.

Her heart labouring, although Ellis had not hurried her in out of the rain, Sorrel stood dripping on his hall carpet, not liking to go into any of the other rooms, if the carpet in any of them was as lush and expensive as the one beneath her feet.

'Your carpet's getting ruined,' she said, raising her eyes from the puddle she was making.

'I'll take half the blame if you'll take the other half,' he said, his terse manner leaving him as his eyes flicked to the puddle of his own making.

And suddenly, when Ellis chose that moment to grin, Sorrel forgot for a brief space, to be on the defensive. And like the sun coming out after so much rain, suddenly she was grinning too.

Unaware as his eyes stared at her that her grin was reflected in the shine of her eyes, when Ellis's face abruptly sobered, a hoarse breath of a whisper involuntarily leaving him that sounded every bit as though she was hearing the words being wrenched from him of, 'God, how I love you!' Sorrel's grin swiftly disappeared.

But even as her eyes started to widen in shock, she knew that she had heard him say nothing of the sort. For there was not so much as a hoarse thread in his voice when, his look as well as his tone matter-of-fact, Ellis said:

'I'm going up to change.' And while her heart had not yet received the message her brain was sending that he hadn't said what she had thought it sounded like, and was giddily misbehaving itself, in a take-it-or-leave-it tone Ellis asked, 'A spare robe of mine or pneumonia?' leaving the choice entirely up to her whether or not she stayed in her wet things.

'Er—do you have a tumble-drier?' she found enough wind to enquire.

It was no help to her idiotic heart to see his grin quirk again, as he said, 'I'm sure I must have—somewhere.'

'Try the kitchen,' she suggested.

But he was already leading her to the stairs. 'I'll do that when I've got your gear.'

Together they squelched up the stairs, Sorrel unable to find one single word to say as he led her along the landing and pushed one of the bedroom doors open, then stood back.

His eyes on her clothes that had become cold as they clung to her, his voice was matter-of-fact again, as he instructed, 'Strip off—I'll throw you in a towel.'

Never more needing to be by herself than at that moment, Sorrel wasted no time in entering through the open door and hastily closing it behind her. Without conscious thought to what she was doing, quickly, like

some wound-up automaton, she obeyed his instruction
to strip off.

Her mind had no room then for anything but, even
though she knew that he hadn't, to wonder crazily if he
had said what so incredulously she had thought for a
split second it had sounded like.

Her thoughts chasing as fast as her fingers, she dropped
her sodden jacket down on to a wide windowsill, her
subconscious designating that area the place less likely
to be ruined than the fine furnishings in the room.

Her fingers went to the buttons on her shirt. Had he
said, 'God, how I love you!' in that hoarse fashion her
ears had picked up? Or was it that with her heart
already playing silly devils to find that, like some
homing pigeon, she had made it to his house in spite of
having no wish to know where he lived, she had
imagined he had said it?

On the point of her imagination she thought, her
shirt following her jacket as she slipped off her shoes
and unzipped her trousers, she had more than sufficient
reason to be wary. Her soaking trousers joining the
bundle on the windowsill, Sorrel was remembering how
at seventeen she had imagined that Ellis had been in
love with her. In fact—a shiver took her as she stood in
her lace-edged coffee-coloured cami-knickers—she had
been certain, sure then, that Ellis loved her. But she had
been mistaken.

It was on the thought that she was not going to be
mistaken a second time, that her imagination must have
a third ear, a totally unsound third ear, especially since
less than a split second afterwards Ellis's voice had been
matter-of-fact rather than hoarse, that Sorrel decided
that since anyway the words had been barely audible,
her ears had played her false.

The next moment she was becoming aware of her surroundings and the scantiness of her attire. And in the next second, as she remembered Ellis saying he would throw her in a towel, Sorrel was sent into utter confusion. For at that moment the door opened, and Ellis came in.

Since she was standing at the opposite side of the room from the door and was taken by stunned immobility, it was left to Ellis to cross the floor to hand her the robe and the towel he had in his hands. But it was when he had come to within a yard of her, the clear light from the window showing the sudden rush of blood to her face, that Ellis froze, and was immobile too.

When an astounded exclamation of, 'Good God!' broke from him, it did nothing to reduce the crimson colour she felt must be staining every part of her body.

No way then could she pretend that she was anywhere near used to men coming up on her when clad only in her underwear that revealed her shapely thighs and her cleavage. And before she could get herself near to being collected, her sophistication stripped from her as she felt stripped, she saw that Ellis was recovering from seeing her blushing as if she was a schoolgirl, and had bent to pick up the soaking bundle from the windowsill.

His back was to her, a gruff note in his voice, as he asked, 'Do you want that thing you have on to be dried?'

'It—it's barely damp,' she replied, her voice choky.

She was glad he did not delay his departure any longer than it took for him to receive her answer. Her limbs suddenly shaky, Sorrel was sorely in need of a sit-down.

Oh, why, why had she had to blush like that? Why had she to go and give herself away like that when it was important that she show him a cool front?

Cross with herself, Sorrel found it more than a little irritating that when she had once lain naked in his arms, his suddenly catching her in her underwear should make her face go a fierce scarlet.

Though, on recalling that she had not been nearly so red-faced when Ellis had held her naked body to him, she saw that on that occasion passion had been there between them. Just now, she was then able to justify, it was no wonder she had blushed—Ellis coming in on her as he had, made it embarrassing that, passion absent, he should see her in nothing but her underwear.

Beginning to wish she had settled for sitting on the back of some hack and was right at this moment at the Pig and Flute lunching with Rod Drury and his relations, Sorrel removed the pins from her hair and began rubbing her hair dry without thought that she hadn't so much as a comb with her.

Oh God! she moaned, when it did dawn on her and she saw the resultant tangle in a dressing table mirror. Neither did she have a lipstick with her. And with the rain not caring that it had denuded her face of make-up, how on earth, the way she was looking now, was she going to show Ellis Galbraith a cool sophisticated outer casing?

To complete her far from sophisticated image, the robe Ellis had handed to her looked to be about ten sizes too big, the shoulders beginning somewhere down the middle of her arms, its hem flapping somewhere below mid-calf.

Groaning anew, she rolled the sleeves back half a dozen times and raked her fingers through her hair to try and make it look somewhere near to being presentable.

Wishing that she had never, in her opinion. so

pathetically weakly allowed him to lead her into his
home, she heard Ellis go by her door and down the
stairs—taking, no doubt, she thought moodily, her
trouser suit and shirt with him.

But that her trouser suit was never going to look the
same again was the least of her worries. Sorrel was
bitterly regretting, for all it was only common sense,
that she had ever parted with it.

She played with the idea of remaining just where she
was until, her trouser suit still warm from the tumble
dryer, Ellis came up to her room with it. He couldn't,
after all, want her there any more than she wanted to be
there, she thought.

For all she knew, he might well have a heavy date
with that blonde this afternoon. She thought about that
for a few moments, of the opinion then that when he
had spotted her standing out in the torrential
downpour, though taking her in and drying her off had
not been in his schedule of things to do that day, but
seeing that she was far from the Drury's home, she had
left him with very little choice but to do what he had.

Another ten minutes ticked by with Sorrel still loath
to leave the room she was borrowing. But, as her nerves
started a violent onslaught that Ellis might be fully
expecting, might now be waiting, for her to go downstairs and join him, so—picturing him sarcastic and
mocking if he took it into his head to come up and ask
what was keeping her—Sorrel jumped up from the bed.

Any sophisticated female would have joined him long
since, she thought. And it was that thought that sent
her out on to the landing.

Though it was with jumping nerves that she made it
down into the hall. Not sure in which room Ellis would
be, or even if she wanted to find him, she stayed in the

hall a further few minutes to admire several of the
superb landscapes adorning the walls.

The sound of a footfall behind her had her jerking
round, the control she wanted coming a second too late
for her to control her jerky movement. Though she did
her best to cover it when she saw that Ellis, in fresh
lightweight sweater and slacks, did not appear exactly
ecstatic that she had decided to come down. But on
remembering the sight she must look to him, any
expression he wore was better than that he should
collapse into helpless laughter at the picture she
presented.

'I came out without a comb,' she tossed at him airily
as, not a word passing his lips, he indicated that she
should precede him into what turned out to be his
drawing room.

Still without a word, Ellis closed the door to the
room, his eyes taking on a speculative light, she
thought, that she had adopted an airy manner which
was at odds with the blushing, choky-voiced woman she
had been upstairs not too long back.

Trepidation started to bite when, silently, he found
her a comb and handed it to her. She knew then that
she had made a mistake in leaving that upstairs room.
But, about to tell him that she would return to that
room upstairs to tidy her hair, suddenly she saw, and
recognised of old, that glint in his eyes that told her he
had something to say and that whether she disappeared
for five minutes, or for however long, she would not be
leaving his house until he had said it.

She clamped nervous fingers hard on the comb in her
hand lest she dropped it, and made herself stand just
where she was to pull the comb through her still damp
tresses. But her eyes were wary on his when, as she

handed the comb back to him, he had still not spoken, but seemed to be waiting until he had her undivided attention.

Not wanting to hear it, whatever it was he had to say, nerves attacked as the comb she had just given him went into his back pocket, so that she was the first to speak. Though without knowing how, she still managed to keep her voice airy, as she said:

'My things are nearly dry by now, I expect?'

'Not quite,' he replied, his tones level, but his eyes fixed on her. 'Sit down, Sorrel,' he added quietly—and added what she had been afraid of: 'I think we might spend the time while waiting in having a little chat.'

Sorrel sat down, purely because if she didn't, he would know for sure that she was all on edge. 'Why not?' she replied, with an insincere smile that from his calculating look she saw didn't cut any ice. 'Your landscapes are quite something,' she said when he too was seated. If they were going to chat a little, then she was determined that she was the one who was going to be in charge of what it was they chatted about. 'Tell me, Ellis,' she went on, intending to enquire about the artists—only she did not get the chance.

'No, Sorrel,' he denied her, 'you tell me,' and giving her no time to try to head him off, whatever it was he wanted to know, 'How come,' he went straight on to ask, 'that with you being so close to this man who pays your rent—this man who pays for your mode of transport and the clothes you wear, apart from that robe you have on, that loving this man dearly, as only last night you told me you do . . .' He paused, but only briefly, his expression stern as with his eyes refusing to let her look away he read the mystification in hers to know what he was getting at; then cleared that mystery for her. But he nearly sank her, when he leaned forward in his chair and ended smoothly, 'Tell me, Sorrel—how come you're still a virgin?'

CHAPTER SEVEN

THOUGH she had been trying to act so cool, Ellis's cool question had made her coolness a non-starter, and sent Sorrel's thoughts darting in all directions. She damned him, as she damned her delay in joining him downstairs. For her reluctance to leave her upstairs sanctuary had, she saw, given him ample time, since she had blushed a fiery red, in which to come to the conclusion he had.

'I'm . . .' she began, halfway to telling him that she was not a virgin. His steady look, that look that said that he knew damn well that she was, stopped her.

'You're——?' he prompted, not, she was sure, endeavouring to help her out, as he asked softly, 'You're not going to tell me otherwise, are you, Sorrel?'

'I wouldn't dream of telling you anything,' she flared, in a corner and not liking it. How did he know? she was asking herself. Her response to him that night, save for that isolated moment when shyness had grabbed her when he had started to admire her naked body, had been all womanly, or so she had thought. But with control coming to her at long last, though she no longer managed to sound airy, 'I'll go and wait upstairs until my things are dry,' she told him.

She had not hung about. But he was at the door before she could get to it, his cool look gone, as in sudden anger, he roared:

'For God's sake *stop running away!*'

'Don't you yell at me!' she fired straight back. 'And . . . and I'm not running away,' she defended.

111

'No?' he questioned, his look tough, but his tone quieter.

'No,' she said tautly. 'I merely thought to let you see, without having to offend you,' she inserted, finding a trace of comfort in sarcasm, 'that I have no wish to answer your personal questions.'

Her sarcasm glanced off him; she doubted it had even touched him. But he was not letting up. Though his voice was once more even, his look steady again, as he asked:

'Personal questions bother you, do they?'

Damning him and his inventor's mind that looked beyond the apparent, and went digging until everything could safely go ahead without the chance of a snarl-up, Sorrel, her attempt to leave frustrated, lost her cool and lost her temper, and in consequence showed him the open wound in her that had never completely healed.

'You have no right to ask personal questions of me,' she blew. 'No right whatsoever!' And, too heated to let him get a word in, her hurt there for him to see, she blazed, 'You gave up any right to ask anything concerning me when you offloaded me eight years ago!'

As soon as she had come to a storming finish, she wanted her words back—there had been just too much pain in that last sentence. She knew that he was aware of that pain too; it was written there in his face, in the way his hand stretched out to her as though he would ease that pain.

Desperately trying to get herself under control, swiftly she turned away. But Ellis, his hands clamping down on her shoulders, made her turn, made her face him as he refused to let her run away, although she was in the same room with him. And with his hands on her, his touch was of no help in her need to find a cool exterior.

'God, how I must have hurt you!' he breathed. And in the next second he was tilting her chin, and she was being made to look at him. There was some emotion in those dark eyes that held hers which she could not fathom, nor was she to fathom, as he told her quietly. 'But there was no other way, Sorrel. You knew how it was with me,' he went on, when she didn't know anything of the sort. 'I could have ended up hating you had I ...'

'Don't lose any sleep,' she deliberately cut him off, ignoring the fact that his mouth had firmed at her offhandedness. His manner of talking to her was making her weak when she could not afford to be weak. She was at pains then that he should not see how very deeply she had been hurt, or how long that hurt had lasted. 'I was over you a long time ago,' she lied.

'You may have got over that hurt, over me,' his short tone came, she knew, from his patience wearing thin rather than from any laughable idea that he didn't like the thought that she had got over him, 'but,' his patience was recaptured, his voice level again, 'it has left a mark on you, hasn't it?' And, not letting her get in this time, 'I was right, wasn't I, Sorrel—you don't trust me, or any other man, an inch, do you?'

Sharply she pulled out of his hold. She'd had it with him, with his questioning. To answer just one question would mean he would have another half a dozen questions queueing up to be voiced.

'I'll live with it,' she snapped. They had come a few yards away from the door, and she took a few rapid steps back to it. But before she could get the door open, he was challenging smartly:

'Why are you in such a tearing hurry?'

Belatedly, she realised that her action in trying to get away from him with all speed was hardly the action of a woman who couldn't care less about him. That such action might be construed as her being fearful of his penetrating questions had her fingers sliding from around the door-handle, her departure delayed as she half turned to tell him:

'I'm in no hurry. It's just that . . .' At that point, she dried up. For Ellis had come up to her and was looking at her with an understanding which she did not understand—until he supplied:

'It's just that you're nervous of me?' And suddenly there was no aggression in him, his tones were almost gentle as, 'But is it me you're nervous of, Sorrel—or yourself?' he asked, his question telling her that she should be racing back to the comparatively safe haven of the Drurys, dressed as she was if need be.

But his voice was again seducing her.

'I . . .' she choked. But as an argument, it didn't even get started.

'Are you afraid that should you find yourself in my arms you'll respond as you did before?' he asked, a question which five minutes ago would have had her agitated and firing up at him, but which now, with his eyes gently hypnotising hers, seemed to nullify all agitation in her. Though he had no need to remind her of the time he was talking of as he went on, 'Like you did that time when that certain naïvety in you should have told me what I saw only today? Are you afraid,' he asked her, his voice gone to be, oh so very quiet, as he made her face her fears. 'that you might in that situation, forget that you have no trust in me, but that if I had you responsive in my arms again, this time you might hold nothing back?'

Mesmerised by him, she seemed to take an age before she could find anything to reply. A mixture of wanting him to stay talking gently to her, to ease her gently into trusting him again, was getting confused with some desperate warning that was trying to make itself heard in her head. What he was suggesting was nothing but the truth of what she was feeling, she had to own. But as for long wordless moments she looked back at him, she saw a danger that she might be weak again. It was then that she sent her confused thoughts seeking to remember how it had been that she had been able to hold back before. And then the memory struggled through of how she had told him she had been playing at responding to him purely to get her own back, at last, albeit that in the face of his non-aggression, there was no anger in her either, and she found her voice to answer only one of his charges.

'You know quite well why I—er—made you believe I was responding to you that time,' she said, trying to stir his anger, needing his anger because the way she was feeling now was not the way she was supposed to feel, and his anger, she thought, would soon give a hiding to the soft wishy-washy person now in charge of her who refused to let the real Sorrel Maitland get through.

'Ah yes,' he agreed, to her dismay with a smile in his eyes, and not a particle of anger to be seen. If anything, his good humour was restored!

'I'd better go,' she tried. 'My things are bound to be dry by now.'

'It's still tipping down outside,' Ellis thought to mention, that smile in his eyes starting to dance, although it was solemnly that he said, 'Even that very fetching undergarment you have on beneath that robe will get soaked if you go out again in this.'

His remark made her pull the crossover fold of the robe a little closer, just as if she thought some of her coffee-coloured lace was showing. And the smile that had begun in Ellis's eyes was suddenly there to quirk his mouth, though the only comment he made was to remind her:

'You know you're not expected back to lunch.'

Sorrel fought a silent battle not to ask the question that hovered on her lips. Fought, and lost. 'What are you suggesting?' she heard the softer person who had taken charge of her ask.

'Nothing more,' he assured her, 'than that you stay and have lunch with me.'

'You—er—don't have a luncheon engagement or anything?' she found herself asking, a picture of the blonde he'd been dancing with last night again popping from nowhere into her head.

'My whole day is at your disposal if you want it,' he offered. And while her world suddenly came alive again as all shades of jealous green got hit on the head, she found that Ellis was actually teasing a smile out of her, when he coaxed, 'Eat with me, Sorrel—I do a fantastic line in cheese sandwiches.'

Her eyes lingered on her curving mouth, obscuring for the moment the reminder that she had brought her own sandwiches. But she had still not said she would stay to lunch when awareness came, and she asked:

'What happened to the packet of smoked salmon and caviare I brought with me?'

'It got soggy,' he replied promptly.

Knowing full well that he was lying, for rain to her knowledge had never yet sogged its way through plastic packaging, suddenly Sorrel wanted to giggle. Though she tried to keep her face straight when, giving in for no other reason than loving him, she did not seem able just then to listen to the sense of what her head would have told her, and murmured:

'One does tend to get a little tired of too much smoked salmon and caviare.'

But she had to smile when a pleased look crossed his face. Though she tried to think nothing of it when, as if he could not help himself, Ellis gave a light kiss to the tip of her nose, for in the next second he was moving from her and growling:

'Any good with a bread knife?'

Unable to find the strength she needed to leave him solitary to eat a cheese sandwich, Sorrel replied, 'The best,' and went with him into the kitchen.

Lunch was not bread and cheese, however, but consisted of tinned soup, steak and salad, followed by cheese and biscuits. To complement one of the best meals she had ever enjoyed went a delicious wine.

Having had more than one or two qualms to start out with as the impervious-to-his-charm person she wanted to be stabbed her with the occasional dart, be it the wine Ellis had served with the meal, or be it his easy manner, Sorrel found she was beginning to feel relaxed.

They had conversed on every subject apart from their two selves. The beautiful landscapes she had seen in the hall had come under discussion. Ellis, she discovered, owned paintings by known and unknown artists, having bought his paintings because he liked them, and not, as with some people she knew, for the impressive name of the artist.

'Had enough?' he asked, when she refused his offer of anything more to eat.

'I shall need that walk back to the Drury's,' she smiled. And, thinking it about time she made tracks back, 'I'll give you a hand with the washing up, then I'll be . . .'

'In the best households, the male of the species reads the paper while the washing up gets done,' he cut her off with a grin.

'So, chauvinist, I'll leave them to drain,' she said, another smile tugged from her at his sauce. But Ellis was right there with her at the sink when she plunged her hands into soapy water.

The washing up, to her mind, was done in record time, and she was soon leaving him to collect her trouser suit from where it had been shaken out after coming out from the tumble-drier, and had been left on a hanger in the hope of the remaining creases falling out of it.

'I can probably run an iron to earth if you want to press it,' said Ellis, following her into the laundry room, and observing the way she was surveying her ruined suit.

'It'll be all right,' she answered, keeping her eyes on her suit. By the sound of it, he was in no hurry for her to go. But common sense ordered that while lunch had gone far better than she would have expected, it had been a self-indulgence on her part which would be better ended.

Though she had to own to feeling just a little piqued that Ellis made no attempt to persuade her to change her mind about staying the half an hour longer it would take to press her suit into any sort of respectability.

Her suit on its hanger in her hand, she moved past him. But before she could exit through the kitchen door, her pride high at the contrary thought that far from trying to delay her, Ellis was trying to get rid of her, her pride was to be mollified when, his voice unhurried, he said:

'Come into the drawing room when you're dressed— I'll have some coffee ready.'

Sorrel went up to the room she had used before, well pleased with the way things had turned out. Not that she had looked for an invitation to share Ellis's lunch. Indeed, had she known at the start of her walk that he would come out of his house and take her in out of the rain, she would never have set out.

She shrugged into her linen trousers, grateful that they had not shrunk, and reflected that what had begun with Ellis firing personal questions, had gone on to be a friendly, if impersonal, lunch where nothing out of the way had been said to upset her.

Knowing that she was likely to hoard the memory to her of the impersonal friendliness she had shared with him when this time of utterly unpredicted self-indulgence was over, she buttoned up her crumpled jacket, and decided to leave her hair down the way it was. A brisk walk across the fields and, with luck, if the Drury clan had not returned, she could go unseen to her room to set about reinstating the person she wanted the outside world to see.

She left the bedroom musing on the point that with her make-up gone, washed off by the rain, for a very brief space of time so too had been washed away the stiffening she had needed for any confrontation with Ellis.

True to his word, he had a tray of coffee waiting when she joined him in the drawing room. He rose to his feet when she entered, but sat down again when she seated herself opposite him.

She smiled at him as he handed her a cup of coffee, thinking that that word confrontation just didn't apply any more. With Ellis being impersonal, she had no need to get uptight. She still felt as relaxed as she had over lunch. Here they were, two civilised people sitting drinking an after-lunch cup of coffee and, given that her suit had seen better days, with Ellis not bringing anything personal into the conversation, civilised was how they were going to remain.

Why then, with Ellis, his long legs stretched out in front of him, looking as relaxed as she was feeling, she should suddenly put paid to the impersonal atmosphere she was enjoying, she could not have said. All she knew was that she could have bitten her tongue out when, with only a few more minutes to go before she would be on her way, it should be she who was the one to start getting personal, by asking him if he liked living in the country, when it was obvious that he did or he would not have bought a house there.

'Neville Drury mentioned that you'd recently moved here,' she ploughed on by way of an explanation for her question.

'I like to get down whenever I can,' Ellis replied smoothly. 'Though my work necessitates my spending a good deal of time in London.'

Having realised her mistake, for any personal discussion about him would surely give him *carte blanche* to ask questions about her, to her alarm, the love she had for him had her unable to deny the need to know more of him than had been written in the press.

'You've certainly got on well since you left Kinglingham,' her wayward tongue pushed on.

But she could have groaned out loud when, not answering the questioning note, she heard that same questioning note in Ellis's voice as, not slow on taking the opening she had given him, suavely he let fall:

'You don't appear to have done so badly yourself.'

If he thought she was rising to that he was mistaken, she thought, starting to get agitated. Determined not to be drawn, she had no reply to make. But in having brought this conversation on herself by getting personal to start with, she was soon being led further down the slippery slope of her own making when Ellis waited no longer for her to make some reply.

'So tell me a little about Sorrel Maitland,' he invited, her look of instant withdrawal not lost on him. But, as if to quiet her fears, as though to suggest that he wasn't so interested that he wanted to hear chapter and verse, he smiled as he said, 'There isn't time now for you to fill in all that's happened in eight years to change you from a beautiful chrysalis into a very beautiful butterfly, but I'll settle for what you did after we—parted company.'

Sorrel had not the least intention of telling him anything. But those last two words had any last remnants of relaxed feeling shooting from her, and made her forget her intentions, as she suddenly erupted wrathfully:

'Parted company! That's a polite way of putting the way you virtually tossed me out on my ear!'

Her flare of anger went as suddenly as it had come. Her only fury then was that she had forgotten herself and had fired up at him. Though Ellis was not replying in kind. Nor was he making any attempt to defend how brutally cruelly he had treated her tender heart. For with his voice quiet, even, he asked softly:

'Does it still matter to you, Sorrel? Does the memory of the way we parted still upset you?'

For several stubborn moments, she refused to answer. But when he remained cool and calm and appeared in no hurry as he deliberately waited for her to come back with something, Sorrel started to see that Ellis Galbraith was no bad hand at psycho-analysis. She saw then how, ever since she had let him see that

isolated moment of hurt to remember how they had
parted company, little by little, by making her relaxed,
at ease, with every friendly word he had spoken, Ellis
had been chipping his way through to the inner Sorrel
Maitland. It was time, more than time, she decided,
that she did something about getting herself together.
Time that she showed him just how little anything to do
with him had the power to upset her.

'No, it doesn't upset me,' she said at length. And she
even managed a self-deprecating smile, as she added, 'I
was in need of a shake-up eight years ago, wasn't I?'
And with another self-deprecating smile, 'No self-
respecting seventeen-year-old has any right to be ...'
her smile wobbled as she faltered, recovered, and tried
again. 'to be that—that ...'

'Innocent? Trusting?' Ellis supplied.

In charge of herself again, Sorrel shrugged. 'If you
like,' she said. And since by the look of him he was
going to insist on hearing more, she forced a light
laugh, as she told him, just as though it was amusing to
remember, 'After you pulled the rug from under my
feet, I went home and did the usual howling my eyes
out.' Her smile became brittle as the memory hit her of
having no recollection of how indeed she had got home
that day. 'Then,' she picked up quickly. 'I decided that
you just weren't worth my tears—I decided instead to
get on with my life.'

That it had been nowhere near as easy as she had
made it sound, that remembering how terrible that time
had been to live through should treacherously weaken
her, and make her resolve to show him a hard front
falter, was soon borne in on Sorrel, when after quickly
dissecting what she had said, Ellis asked:

'You came to London straight away?'

'Not immediately,' she had answered before she had given herself time to think. 'I was . . .' She halted, wishing she had agreed that yes, she had come to London straight away. Too late now that she had told him she had not done so, to change her story. But to lie and tell him that she had gone straight from his employment into the employ of Cynthia Armitage brought her up short to realise that that could have him asking questions which she just did not want him to ask. Live without his love she could, but to live with the contempt he would show her when he unhesitatingly put her in the same stable as Wenda Sykes was something in her new-found resurgence of love for him which she could not take.

Having been lost in her thoughts, Sorrel was miles away from remembering that she had broken off halfway through a sentence. But Ellis quietly prompting, when she did not look like resuming, 'Go on, Sorrel,' made her rapidly leave thoughts of how blacker than black Cynthia Armitage would make it sound if Ellis ever got to hear her tell it.

'I—er . . .' she began, agitated that he should not know anything about her being a nanny, or about the quite ghastly daughter dear old Mr Ollerenshaw had managed to sire, she fell down in her desire that Ellis should know nothing either of how things had been with her when he had so summarily dismissed her. 'I was ill for a time,' she said, and barely knew she had said it, until his cool even manner left him, and Ellis, his face showing his surprise, exclaimed:

'You were *ill*!'

'Oh, nothing serious,' she replied, of no mind to tell him of the rapid weight loss that had gone with her total loss of appetite, or of those days spent staring into space with just him in her head, of those sleepless nights where he still filled her mind, and which had resulted in her looking so ill that her mother had taken her to see a doctor.

Unaware of the pain that filled her expression at her thoughts, Sorrel came away from memories she did not want, but only to be weakened again by the concern on Ellis's face, as with a frown grooving his forehead, he asked:

'What was the trouble?'

She sighed, thinking that at least they had passed the danger area of Cynthia Armitage, but not liking at all that he was still applying pressure.

'I'll see you have a doctor's report,' she said with quiet sarcasm. But she was not, she saw, going to be let off the hook. For Ellis took no heed of her sarcasm, as he said:

'You never had need to use the medical fraternity during the time I knew you. So despite what you say, it must have been something serious.'

'It wasn't,' she denied, getting fed up with him and his badgering away at her. 'If you must know,' she said heatedly, only the fact of his accusing her of running away keeping her there, pride demanding that instead of walking out right there and then she stick this out until he had got tired of it, 'if you must know,' she repeated snappily, 'I was ...' Again she faltered. But she was grabbing at her courage as anger went, leaving her voice husky. 'I was in a bit of a mess—emotionally.'

There, she'd got it out. Let him make of it what he would. Sorrel at that moment began to recover, and then did not care a defiant damn what he thought.

Though the shocked breath she heard from his chair told her that whatever ailments which she might have

suffered that had gone through his head, that he had
been the cause of her needing to see a doctor, had never
occurred to him. It was there showing in his expression
when she looked at him. A stunned look was there the
moment before the utterly appalled words left him:

'You had a—*breakdown*!'

It made her angry then that when he had slammed
the door shut on the love she had told him she bore
him, he should think her love had been such a poor
thing that she could take his harsh rejection of all she
had offered, without it affecting her. And she was on
her feet, her anger spilling over, out of her control as
she yelled at him;

'Dammit, you were my world—I *loved* you!'

Before the ring of her words had faded, Ellis was out
his chair too. Her sophistication vanished when, her
emotions on a see-saw, he took her trembling form in
his arms.

'Oh God, I never knew,' he groaned, some emotion
in him too, as his cheek against her cheek, he breathed,
'I never knew you loved me that much.'

She had told him, Sorrel thought, anger surging
upward again. She had *told* him how it was with her.
'You knew,' she accused hotly, pulling her cheek away
from his, her eyes hostile. 'But you decided it was just
kid's stuff.' She had a clear picture of that morning
when he had sacked her and had walked coldly from
her, and had left her absolutely shattered standing
there. 'You knew, but you didn't care what went on
inside me,' she threw at him. 'You . . .' A dry choking
sob caught at her unexpectedly, and she broke off.

Ellis bringing her head down to his shoulder, cradling
her to him, whispering, 'Hush, darling,' in such a gentle
way, made Sorrel pull back her head, her eyes full of

unshed tears. And again Ellis was gently kissing her, as last night he had kissed her, his kiss beautiful, as though he would draw from her all the pain he had inflicted.

A sigh shuddered through her when his lips left hers, but his kiss had had some healing effect in that her temper had gone, her anger had gone. But still within the circle of his arms, she felt her world right itself again, and albeit she drew a shaky breath, she was then able to mumble:

'I never meant to—tell you any—of that.' Her voice went to be a whisper as, looking away from him, she added, 'I wish I hadn't.'

'Don't,' he said promptly, one hand coming to stroke down her cheek. 'I'm glad I know.'

'Why?' she asked, her solemn eyes returning to his.

As solemnly, Ellis looked back at her. Quietly then he answered, 'I've only recently started to see what I should have seen a long time ago. Your eyes were always laughter-filled in the old days—it wasn't until we met up again and that laughter had gone from your beautiful eyes that I started to see what you're at pains to keep hidden.'

Her heart starting to pound, Sorrel lowered her eyes so that he should read nothing more there. Was he saying that he had seen that she loved him? She was ready to deny all charges as she asked the diverting question:

'What have my eyes, laughing or otherwise, got to do with what I've told you?'

'They reveal a sensitivity you try to hide,' he answered unhesitatingly. 'A sensitivity which in those days of my having my sights pinned on succeeding in the business world, cravenly, I missed seeing.' She felt calmer as she realised that he had missed seeing how much he meant to her now. 'What you've just told me,' he went on, 'has given me a further insight into just how very great is that depth of sensitivity in you, Sorrel.'

Sorely then did she need some trite remark. But in the absence of being able to find anything killing, she was of the opinion that Ellis could no longer accuse her of running away if she left now.

She made a move to pull out of his arms, and when he let her go without making her struggle to be free, she was able to tell him:

'I'm not that sensitive any longer, Ellis.'

She did not like that small shake of his head, any more than she liked his correcting statement. 'What you mean is that you don't want me or any other man to see sensitivity in you. But it's still there, as fragile and as deep as ever.'

From the smile in his eyes she saw that he did not need a reply. He knew, and no amount of her denying it would convince him otherwise. She settled for a different tack.

'I no longer love you, if that's what you're trying to suggest,' she lied coldly. But she wondered, a shade panicky, if Ellis knew she was lying when his hands came to rest on her shoulders, keeping her there, as he asked:

'But you don't hate me either, do you?'

For a second or two she contemplated telling him that she felt dead inside where he was concerned. But, remembering her heated response to his lovemaking that night in her flat, remembering his smile, his 'Ah yes,' when she'd tried to reiterate that her response was only put on, she had more than a little idea that he wouldn't swallow that.

She tried one of her practised dismissive shrugs, and was offhand as she told him, 'How can I hate you, Ellis? Without you, it would have taken years for the little village girl to grow up.'

His hands tightened on her shoulders as a glint suddenly appeared in his eyes at her display of arrogance. 'You're laying the charge—the responsibility—at my door for the phoney image you present to the world?' he asked, not, she guessed, at all enamoured with her phoney image.

For a bonus she gave him one of her phoney practised smiles. But she was admitting he was responsible for nothing, when, pulling away from him a second time, her laughter tinkled as she told him:

'If you don't like the image, Ellis, I can think of half dozen or more men who do.'

That should kill stone dead any glimmer that might have come to him of where her heart lay, she thought. She would have gone strolling casually to the door then had he not halted her, no trace of anger there that the glint in his eyes denoted, when he asked smoothly:

'That includes the man who pays your rent, does it?'

Wanting to be gone, Sorrel repressed a puckering of her brow as she wondered what thoughts were going through his head now. But her false smile was still there as, 'Naturally,' she agreed.

Sorrel did not like at all that, as phoney smiles went, the one that Ellis favoured her with then beat hers into a cocked hat. And smooth wasn't the word for the way he sardonically let the words fall:

'Let us hope, my dear Sorrel, that the gent has the patience he's going to need while he waits until you're prepared to give him what he's paying for.'

As a snide remark to her still virgin state, Sorrel did not think much of it. Her head was high in the air when, seeing there was nothing more to be said, she sailed haughtily to the door.

CHAPTER EIGHT

WHEN Rod Drury drove her back to London on Sunday, Sorrel was never more glad to return to the solitude of her flat. She desperately needed time to be by herself to think.

Ellis had insisted on driving her back to the Drurys' yesterday, but she had been in no mind to have any sort of further conversation with him—he, for once, had been like-minded. He had dropped her off with barely another word passing between them, and she had hurried to her room to change out of her never-to-be-the-same-again trouser suit. And no sooner had she repaired the ravages of her day and was once again looking more like the girl she had set out to be, than Rod and his family were back, Rod coming straight to her room to enquire with some concern whether she, like them, had got caught out in the rain.

'Rainwater's good for the complexion,' she had remarked lightly, her meeting with Ellis and all that had followed already secreted away in a very private compartment.

'Your complexion doesn't need any help,' Rod had replied, his eyes serious, troubled, so that for a moment she worried that he might be as deeply hurt as she had been by not having a love returned. But he had smiled then, and had told her, 'Everybody's gone full pelt to take baths. There'll be no hot water left by now. Come and talk to me while the steam builds up again.'

After that, it seemed that she hadn't had a minute to

herself in which to try and get her thoughts together. For half an hour later she and Rod were joined in the drawing room by Moira Drury. When he had gone to take his bath, it had not been deemed polite to just get up and return to her room.

Then more relatives had trickled in, and by the time Sorrel had thought that she could decently make it to her room, Rod, having had the quickest bath on record, she was sure, was bathed and changed and had come to sit on the arm of her chair, and, by now sensitive to that troubled look in his eyes, she was loath to make him look in any way discomfited by straight away getting up and leaving the room.

More than pleased with the way the staff had coped last night, Moira and Neville Drury had decided to give them a breather on Saturday night by taking their guests en masse out to dinner. And with more champagne flowing, and no one in any hurry to leave the hotel that had been chosen for their repast, it was gone midnight when they all returned to the house.

By that time the emotions of the day, notwithstanding having to act as though she had nothing more important on her mind than what she might wear tomorrow, had left Sorrel quite exhausted with keeping her end up, and she went to bed too mind-weary to get her thoughts into any sort of shape.

Sunday had started out as damply as Saturday had turned out to be, and with people housebound, although Sybil would have taken off like a shot had anyone suggested a ride, it again seemed to Sorrel that she would be being impolite if she stayed up in her room for any length of time.

Resigned to the fact that any thinking she had to do would have to be left until she got home, she was

relieved when not long after lunch, Rod told his parents
that they would be on their way.

With everyone coming out to wave them off, Moira's
sincere, 'I'm so glad you were able to come,' made
Sorrel wonder as she thanked her for an enjoyable
weekend—not totally a lie, for the Drurys were a
happy family—if Moira knew the doubt that they
would meet again, and half an hour seemed to pass
before Rod set the car in motion.

She was glad to reach her flat. Though before she
could be left alone with her thoughts, first Rod insisted
on escorting her right to her door.

'You've enjoyed the weekend as much as you told my
mother you had?' he asked the moment they had halted,
that same serious troubled look there she had seen
before.

'Your family are lovely people,' she told him quietly.
'It was very nice meeting them all.'

'You could meet them all again if you wanted to,'
said Rod quickly. 'We could . . .' The sadness that came
to her eyes made him break off. 'You meant it when
you said it wouldn't have done any good had I waited a
while to ask you to marry me?'

'Yes, I did,' she answered—kinder by far, she
thought, to give him a straight answer than to skate
around the issue.

Though he was still not quite ready to let go, she
found. For he was speedily then reminding her of how
he had kept his promise that they would be good pals
only that weekend and nothing more, adding:

'We could go on being good pals, Sorrel. I haven't
chased you this weekend. I wouldn't . . .'

'No, Rod,' she had to tell him. 'It—wouldn't work.'

Remembering her own dreadful heartache when at

seventeen she had been made to realise that she would never see her love again, she very nearly weakened and said that she would see him occasionally, but instinct stopped her. Somehow she instinctively knew that the love Rod had for her was not the all-consuming fire of feeling she had for Ellis.

'It's better this way,' she told him as gently as she could.

Sure in her own mind as she was that she had never given Rod any reason to suppose that she felt anything as deep as love for him, her heart was heavier than ever when eventually she parted from him.

A sigh escaped her as she closed the door of her flat, remembering the last time Rod had seen her home. But this time, if Ellis did not physically follow her in, he was there in her thoughts and was to immediately leave no room for unhappy thoughts of Rod Drury.

By nine the next morning Sorrel had just about done with berating herself for the crass, idiotic, most stupidly self-indulgent person she had been from almost the moment Ellis had come from his house and seen her standing there in the pouring rain. As if he had been calling her all along—which just had to be another piece of self-indulgence that she could think such a thought, even while telling herself she would avoid walking near any house lest it be his—she had found her way to his home.

But this morning she was done with self-indulgence, and any other indulgence too. While Ellis had her phone number and knew where she lived, even while she told herself umpteen times that he would not be contacting her, she was fully aware that the ring of the phone or a ring at her flat bell would send her first thoughts flying to think that it might be him.

It had occurred to her halfway through the night that merely to have her telephone number changed would achieve nothing. Ellis would still know where she lived. It had been getting on for five in the morning when what she had to do became clear to her.

At five past nine, Sorrel telephoned the agents responsible for leasing her her flat, and asked them to sub-let it for her. At ten past nine, she left her flat and was on her way to see other flat-leasing agencies.

Money, she was discovering again, was a very useful commodity. What she was looking for was a more modest type of apartment, the type of apartment that a working girl could afford.

'It's like looking for gold,' said the third agent she visited, as if she didn't already know that. But, as his shrewd eyes dwelt on her expensive clothes, he considered her for a few more seconds, then said, 'Though if you can cough up a year's rent in advance, I might have something on my books.'

Ready to snatch his hands off, Sorrel told him that a year's rent in advance should not provide too much of a problem, and she was then given details of the flat the agent had up his sleeve.

When he described the small one-bedroomed flat, she was ready to take it sight unseen. But with his promise that he would hold it for her, she took the keys and went hurrying round to what she was sure was going to be her new abode.

It was a small flat, as he had said, but it was fairly presentable, so that she could see nothing against her moving in straight away. She could take her time about changing the wallpaper, she thought, and hurried back to the agent to tell him she would have it. That her new flat was in a less salubrious area than the one she was living in mattered not a jot to her.

Speed to her mind was essential then—she had a lot to do. Fortunately, since while the flat had no tenant its owner was not receiving rent, no objection was raised to her signing a tenancy agreement that day.

Finding a removal firm who could transfer sufficient of her furniture to make her new abode comfortable was the hardest part, she found. Though when fast growing of the opinion that she would have to buy a camp bed since she was determined to be in her new flat by the weekend, she finally managed to run to earth a two-man band who said they would do the job on Friday afternoon.

The next few days saw Sorrel, when she wasn't running up new curtains, feverishly packing and itemising all she would be taking with her. That some of her furniture would have to stay behind was of no great consequence. If her tenant, when found, didn't want to take it over, then she would sell it.

When the removal men turned up not at two o'clock as promised, but at gone three on Friday afternoon, Sorrel was so relieved to see them that the ticking off she had been building up to give them went completely from her mind.

'Leave the things in the bedroom until last,' she told the wiry man who seemed to be the senior of the two. She had no wish to teach them their job, but to her mind, and with time going on, if her bed was the last article to be loaded, it would then have to be the first off. She was going to be whacked at the end of this day, and to have her comfortable bed set up was a first priority.

Sorrel closed her eyes to chipped paintwork and a

scratched table, as in and out of her flat the two men heaved and bumped.

They had just gone out carrying her settee between them, when in no time she heard the sound of one of them returning.

'That was . . .' As she turned, the word 'quick' died in her throat.

To see Ellis Galbraith standing in her doorway, his eyes flicking round the room and coming to a stop when he saw the matching two chairs to the settee he had most likely just seen being carried to the removal van parked outside, made her wish furiously that the removal men had arrived at the time they had stated. It might all have been done by now. She might well have been in her new flat—Ellis would never have known that she had gone.

Unspeaking, she surveyed him as he came further into the room, her composure returning as she realised he might know that she was moving, but there was no way he was going to know her new address.

She was hopeful that since she had nothing to say, he might state the nature of his business. But, recalling that he never had yet given her any reason for why he had called, she was not too surprised that his opening remark should tell her nothing, save that he hadn't needed to stir himself to gather what was going on.

'Doing a flit?' he enquired, his expression bland in the face of her not looking very pleased to see him.

'I don't owe rent,' she told him waspishly. But she could see from the way he propped himself up against the back of an easy chair, the way he looked at her with one eyebrow ascending, that some comment she wasn't going to like would very shortly be coming her way.

'But you owe your—landlord—don't you, Sorrel?'

And, not done with his insolent questions, a taunting light had come to his eyes, when not waiting for a reply, he mocked, 'Get fed up with waiting for you to come across, did he?'

'You . . .' she started to bite, then heard the two removal men coming back. 'I'm busy,' she snapped, of no mind to have a verbal set-to with other ears present. 'If you've got something concrete to say, say it and . . .' She broke off as the removal men came into the room.

But she realised that Ellis didn't care who overheard what he said, as he took the risk of her not being so sensitive that she wouldn't scorch his ears with something acid in front of anyone listening. For, looking urbanely unruffled, he obliged by deigning, on this occasion, to tell her why, so untimely, he had arrived at her flat.

'I called to ask you to have dinner with me tonight,' he said pleasantly; his pleasant look staying although he had his answer in the sour look she threw him.

'You have . . .' She stopped, the removal men looking at the two of them with open interest making her falter. It just wasn't in her then to reply, only to have Ellis come back with something which he wouldn't care if it embarrassed her or not. 'Come into the bedroom,' she told him, and could have killed him when, her only thought having been to get him out of earshot of the others, he murmured charmingly:

'Now there's an invitation I won't refuse!'

Furious with him, not seeing anything at all as funny as the smirking witnesses obviously did, Sorrel marched stormily into her bedroom and left him to follow or not as he pleased.

She was in no mood to dress it up when the sound of her bedroom door closing told her that he had indeed

taken up her invitation. And she was in no mood at all
to sweetly turn down his, as she swung round to face
him. In her view this should not have taken half a
minute. She did not waste a second, but launched in
straight away with:

'In case you haven't yet got the picture, Ellis
Galbraith, I'll clarify the position for you. I . . .'

'This sounds as though it's going to be good,' he
commented to interrupt her flow when she had just
built up a fine head of steam.

'It will be,' she said tartly, 'when you realise that for
my part, I can do very well without seeing you again.'

His expression was still relaxed, his manner easy still,
but Sorrel did not miss the slight momentary narrowing
of his eyes, before he suggested softly:

'Scared, Sorrel?'

She swallowed down more wrath that he had so
effortlessly hit on that conclusion, and aimed a
broadside at him to try to deflect any other conclusions
he might reach.

'Unusual though I'm sure it is for you to receive the
big "E", Ellis, you'll just have to face it—you're just
not every female's idea of a knight on a white charger!'

It annoyed her intensely that instead of accepting
gracefully that she had no wish to go out with him, Ellis
should rock back on his heels as he favoured her with a
thoughtful look that made her dearly want to know
what he was thinking. She didn't like his second
conclusion any better than she had liked the first.

'You're still doing it.'

'Doing what?' she snapped back, but wished she
hadn't when he replied:

'Running away.'

'I'm n . . .' About to deny the charge, she halted, then

shrugged indifferently. 'If that's the way you want to see my moving,' she said, and could have gasped at her own stupidity.

For the shaken look that had come to him, the 'My God!' that left him, before he said, stunned, 'You're not moving flat just because I happen to know where you live!' told her that he had not been accusing her of physically running away from him, but of running away from any conversation with him that might go into areas which she did not want to face.

Sarcasm was her only defence. Airily she let her eyes skim over him, hardening her heart at the weakness just having him with her evoked.

'I believe, Ellis,' she drawled, 'that I may have mentioned your colossal conceit before.'

But again she was to find that any attempt she made to cut him down to size was a non-starter. For as he recovered from the thought that he might be the reason for the removal van being outside, Sorrel saw that her sarcastic dart had not found its mark. The cool smile that was on his mouth told her that, as he challenged:

'It goes without saying, of course, that you were going to let me know your forwarding address.'

Sorrel had quite a line in insincere smiles herself. She selected one now, even as she thought 'over my dead body'. 'Of course,' she told him sweetly. 'Your name is right at the top of my mailing list.'

His smile became genuine as amusement at her sarcasm briefly quirked the corner of his mouth. But his mouth had straightened, his eyes steady on hers as he suggested, 'Since I'm here, I'll save you the postage.'

Like hell he would! she thought. No way was she going to do as he was asking and give him her new address. She rather thought he knew that anyway, for he waited no longer than a couple of seconds before he was on to another gambit.

'Does the boy-friend get to know where you're going?'

'Rod Drury, do you mean?' she asked in reply, needing a breather to assess what tack he was on now.

'Safety in numbers?' he came back, reading her answer as meaning that she had more than one boy-friend.

She didn't like his way of putting that question, any more than she liked the question itself, or any of this conversation.

'I shan't be seeing Rod Drury again,' she told him flatly, wishing he would go. All was quiet in the other room again, and she wanted to go and check that a piece of furniture that wasn't supposed to go had not just been carted out. Though she did find a small relief that Ellis could not be so convinced it was on account of himself that she was moving, when he said quietly:

'You thought it kinder to move than to give him any hope that you would marry him?' Sorrel looked at him, hoping her face was as expressionless as she was trying to make it. Then she saw him smile, as with some charm he said, 'You must have quite a list of old addresses.'

She did not miss the implication that he thought many men must have asked her to marry them and that she moved on every time someone got turned down. But that his remark should amuse her was unexpected, and she lowered her eyes lest Ellis, with his sharp perception, saw laughter there. Then, once more in control, she looked across at him, and had the hardest work in the world not to match his grin when sourly she told him:

'You're getting very free with your compliments,

Galbraith.' She turned her back on him and walked to
the window, just the fact of him being there wearing
down her resistance. 'I'm very busy,' she told him
tonelessly, refusing to look at him again as she hoped
he would take the hint.

'Having dinner with me tonight?' he asked, his tone
light.

'No, thanks,' she replied, her back to him, her fingers
gripping hard on to the windowsill. All was silent in the
room, a silence that stretched. Soon Ellis would go
without knowing where it was that she was going, and
never would he know how much she wanted to go with
him anywhere he asked.

What was in his mind as he stood without saying a
word, she had no idea. But when his deep voice
suddenly broke the silence, and he said, 'Be happy,' she
knew that those two words were his way of saying that
he had accepted that she did not want to see him again.

She did not move away from the window when the
door of the bedroom opened and then quietly closed
after him. And unshed tears were in her eyes as his last
footsteps died away. Oh God, how much she loved him!

Ellis did not look up to the window when he stepped
outside the building. And Sorrel had all the evidence
she needed that the prospect of not seeing her again had
less than little the crippling effect that knowing she
would not see him again had on her. For as one of the
removal men admired Ellis's Jaguar parked next to the
van, Ellis stopped to have a word, and though she could
not hear what remarks passed between the two men, she
was sure it was some goodhumoured banter when the
sound of masculine laughter floated back up to the
open window.

She was feeling fairly frazzled when at long last she

was able to say goodbye to the men who had moved her furniture, and closed the door of her new apartment. Though having her furniture placed more or less where she wanted it, and moving in, did not end there.

But by the time she had unpacked and found homes for china, cutlery and cooking utensils, her nerve-ends had quietened. She even started to feel hungry as she undid the first of her suitcases and started to hang her clothes away. But if having found that by beavering away she was getting to feel better about having parted from Ellis a final second time, or so she told herself, Sorrel was not of a mind to get herself something to eat, when the time spent sitting down and disposing of anything she prepared would give Ellis free rein to take over her thoughts again.

Determined as she had to be not to dwell on thoughts of him, she concentrated her thoughts on the totally emancipated woman she was going to be. The sophisticated image she had adopted for a while had never been her anyway. What she must aim for now was something in between the still gullible person she knew she would always be deep down, and that aloof person who had never been quite her. Dear old Mr Ollerenshaw had meant her to have a good time, and she had tried, so from that point of view she was sure he would rest easy in his grave. But, basically, she was not happy with having nothing to do.

Try as she would, Ellis insisted on not staying out of her thoughts for very long, as she remembered the 'Be happy', he had wished her. Well, she would be happy, she vowed. She was tougher now than she had been at seventeen. She would take a secretarial refresher—things were bound to have changed in the office world these last eight years—but she had been good at her job before, and she would be again.

The thought jumped into her head from nowhere that she had probably been good at her job purely because it had been such a great joy to her each morning to go to work; to see Ellis; to do all she could to take the pressure off him and so leave him more time for more important work.

Ousting Ellis from her thoughts again, the last of her clothes put away, Sorrel left her bedroom and pinned her thoughts determinedly on the career girl she was going to be; on the enjoyment she was sure she would find again in office work, regardless of whom was her boss.

But although her sights were once more set on the fully emancipated woman she would be, she was to fall at the first hurdle. For finding, when she went to place anything on it, that the kitchen shelf had decided to give up the ghost, only just rescuing her coffee percolator before it went sliding into the sink, she was to discover that it wasn't any good to just push the few screws back and pray that they held—because they didn't.

Not knowing one end of a screwdriver from another, even if she'd had one, she remembered that Rod Drury had left a handful of something he called Rawlplugs which he'd popped out for on her last moving day. She was sure she had seen them somewhere.

Recognising that she had been totally and unpretentiously feminine on that occasion, with no Rod Drury there to help her this time, Sorrel refused to be beaten.

Running the Rawlplugs to earth, she tried first with a nail file and then with a knife to embed the screws further and more securely into the wall.

Frustration, a bent nail-file and a chipped knife later, Sorrel was near to admitting defeat. She was in the middle of owning that where it seemed second nature for the mere male to accomplish such jobs, she was making not the smallest headway, when the new sound of her door bell made her jump.

Her hair scraped back in a rubber band, her many times washed jeans unearthed and changed into as soon as the removal men had departed, an unsophisticated Sorrel went to the door. She was of a mind then that should her caller, probably a neighbour come to say hello to a newcomer, be of the male variety, then without compunction she was going to haul him in and if need be use helpless feminine wiles to cajole him into making that shelf secure for her.

But shock was to leave her speechless the moment she had her door open. For as Ellis Galbraith's eyes swept from her hair with its stray waving wisps over her T-shirt and shabby jeans, she was sure she had never looked scruffier. She was of the opinion then that, having thought he had most likely found some other female to take to dinner or that he had journeyed back to his home in Kent, her shelf could stay down for ever more as far as she was concerned.

'How the . . .' she managed to gasp, when shock left her vocal cords a little free.

'Now now,' said Ellis cheerfully, a delicious-smelling paper-wrapped parcel in one hand, a bottle of wine in the other. 'You wouldn't swear at a Samaritan who thought to ask the removers where they were taking your stuff and, in case you can't find your plates, has brought you something we can eat out of the paper, would you?'

When she had been at such pains not only to move her address but to keep her new address from him, only to have him so simply outsmart her, Sorrel was ready to more than swear. But that was before Ellis gave her the benefit of the wickedest grin yet, and then coaxed, just as though he had seen her nose twitching at the aroma emanating from the parcel he held:

'Give in, Sorrel—you know you're starving.'

Admitting he had for the time being outfoxed her, her reserves of strength did not, in that moment of having to make a decision, have time to build themselves up. Though it was with not much welcome that she opened the door wider. And it was quite belligerently that she asked him:

'Are you any good with a screwdriver?'

CHAPTER NINE

THE refixing of Sorrel's kitchen shelf had to wait. With Ellis declaring that he was starving too, and that he had no intention of eating cold fish and chips, she quickly cleared the kitchen table of impedimenta, and warmed two plates under the hot tap, while he hunted around for a couple of wine glasses.

Though he found the wine glasses, a corkscrew proved elusive. 'I'll show you an old Boy Scout trick,' Ellis told her charmingly, when she had been determined not to be charmed.

By dint of an attachment to his penknife, he had the wine bottle uncorked while Sorrel was trying to get over the mental picture of him as a boy in Scout's uniform. She clamped down hard when her imagination strayed to seeing a picture of a son they had produced between them following in his father's footsteps.

Ellis's manner throughout the makeshift meal was companionable and easy, so that by the time quantities of fish and chips had been consumed, Sorrel was desperately trying to tell herself that it was nothing more than the Muscadet which he had brought to go with the fish that was responsible for the never-more-alive feeling that had surged in her.

But it was on facing the fact that she would still be feeling this way had it been plain water she had been drinking that she had to put a check on what she was feeling—this unexpected time with him was not conducive to her being the strong person she had to be, not only now, but when he had gone.

As soon as his plate was empty, she was on her feet. 'It's getting late,' she hinted as she collected up the things they had used and took them to the draining board.

She heard the scrape of his chair, and could do nothing about the drumming of her heart as, much too close, he stood near and murmured in her ear:

'Would I leave a lady in distress?'

Her thoughts flew back to that day he had walked from her and left her broken without so much as a backward glance. You did once, she thought painfully, but her face was composed when she took a side step from him, then turned to look at him. But Ellis was not looking at her, but at the lopsided shelf.

'I can get it fixed tomorrow,' she said, her need that he should go at odds with her wanting him to stay.

'I don't like loose ends,' he said softly, and suddenly he was looking at her with quiet waiting eyes.

His look, his waiting, made Sorrel tense all at once. Up until a few moments ago his relaxed manner had been rubbing off on to her—but no longer. There in his eyes she saw a quality that belied the fact that his remark had been a throwaway one. He's asking me to trust him, she thought, and knew it for a fact as tension grew taut in her. In that moment, she knew that his look, his saying that he didn't like loose ends, all added up to mean that he wanted her to trust him—to trust him enough to tie up the loose ends he did not know about her!

That tension in her threatened to snap as she realised that to give him the trust he was silently asking for would mean trusting him enough to fill in such details as—who had paid the rent on her last flat.

Abruptly she broke the hold he had on her eyes. Tearing her eyes from his, all she knew then was that she could not bear that his look of wanting her trust should change into one of searing contempt, should she tell him any of it.

'Well,' she said, her voice quiet as she controlled the sick sensation that had invaded her insides, 'since the only reason I let you in was so you could put that loose-ended shelf back for me, I wouldn't dream of stopping you—if you insist.'

She ignored that his dark eyes were still on her, and turned back to the sink, praying with all she had that he would leave it at that. She had started to wash up when, aware of his every movement, she heard him leave the kitchen.

She heard him go out through her flat door, and was in the throes of thinking that he had grown fed up with trying to reach her and that, without so much as a goodbye, he had gone. But when she was just about to give in to the feeling of wanting to collapse, she heard him returning. She was rapidly having to draw on every remains of what strength she had left.

Though to see that Ellis had regained his previous easy manner when he came into the kitchen enabled her to gain her second wind.

'In the absence of a screwdriver,' he commented casually, holding aloft some alien-looking metal implement which he had obviously been to his car to collect, 'we'll follow the advice of Confucius.'

'Which was?' she asked, striving for a light note.

'When screwdriver not to hand, use your loaf,' quoted Ellis in a Chinese accent that was so excruciatingly awful, she was sure no self-respecting Chinese would own to it.

Having jumped from one emotion to another, to find that now tension had gone, she wanted to giggle, Sorrel was not quick enough in straightening the amused curve of her mouth as she said solemnly:

'I doubt that screwdrivers had been invented in Confucius's day.'

A smile was on Ellis's mouth as his eyes stayed on her mouth. 'Wretched woman,' he said softly, 'do you dare to doubt the authenticity of my quotation?'

'As if I'd call you a liar!' she returned, and was so overcome then with a feeling of wellbeing, of enjoying their ridiculous banter, that she knew that great gaping cracks were going to appear in the hard nut of the person she had to be, if she didn't watch it. 'I've got some things to do in my bedroom,' she said, quickly drying her hands the sooner to reach her refuge.

Her control falling apart, she took no heed of him staring at her as, trying not to break into a run, she hurried past him to her bedroom. All was silent in the kitchen as minutes passed while she fought to get herself under control.

But only when she heard noises coming from the kitchen that told her that the next time she presented herself there would find her shelf level once more, did she start to get herself more of one piece.

Not intending to risk the close proximity with him undermining her again, she stayed where she was. Ellis would call to her when he had finished, she thought, and only then would she join him. All that would be required then would be a thank-you for the job he had done, a polite thank-you for her supper, then if he showed no sign of being in any hurry to go, she would plead tiredness and bid him goodnight.

It did not work out quite the way she had planned it.

For one thing, straightening the errant shelf took less time than, since she had been attempting it herself for an age, she had calculated. And Ellis did not call her into the kitchen to admire his handiwork, but came to her bedroom, not to tell her to come and look, but to stand in the doorway and say:

'Come and tell me where you want your pictures hung—I saw some on the occasional table in the living room.'

'I—er . . .' Her control wavered at the thought that he seemed in no hurry to leave her. But he must leave, she thought; she just could not take very much more of this—this—intimate togetherness. 'It's—late to start knocking picture hooks in the walls,' she managed, and even put together a smile, as she added, 'I don't want my neighbours hating me before I've introduced myself!'

She bent then to smooth the cover of her bed which was already smooth, and gained another morsel of control. But she very nearly split asunder, shock hitting her, when straightening suddenly, she was caught breathless to see Ellis quietly watching her—with a look of love for her in his eyes!

Aware that that had to be her craziest notion yet, Sorrel looked quickly from him, her control all over the place as she stammered:

'It—it's late. Y-you'd better go.'

She dared another look at him, and knew how idiotic she had been to think she had seen love for her there. For his eyes were showing only good humour, not even affection, as he calmly remarked:

'If you were a lady, you'd invite me to spend the night . . .' his eyes flicked to the bed, 'on that . . .' he paused, the devil suddenly lighting his eyes at her tense frosty look, 'on that settee out there,' he ended, which she was sure had certainly not been what he had started out to say.

His grin was suddenly her undoing. For no way could she avoid the matching grin that broke from her at his devilment. 'If I could be sure I would have a perfect gentleman sleeping on my settee—who knows,' she said, laughter in her eyes, 'I might have been tempted.'

Her laughter faded when, his manner easy again, Ellis left his position by the doorway and came to put an arm about her shoulders. Just his touch she felt weakening, but she was to hear that it would soon be over when, casually, he said:

'Walk with me to the door.'

Unable to make any comment that wouldn't come out sounding choky, Sorrel went to her flat door with him, Ellis's arm still about her. She wanted then, with a burning ache within her, to rest her head against him. She was still fighting with all she had not to give in to the impulse when he broke the silence that had been briefly between them.

'I'll hang those pictures tomorrow,' he said, humour still with him as he added, 'I'll arrive early.'

But Sorrel shook her head. The moment she had known since seeing him at the door would come was there. She had to end it now—for the sake of her peace of mind she could not afford to duck it. She took a step back and out of the semi-circle of his arm. She did not want his touch to weaken her when she said what she must.

'I—don't want to see you again, Ellis,' she told him quietly, and hoped with all she had that he would understand. Running away he might call it, but she just could not keep changing her flat every five minutes, yet that would be the only option open to her if he refused to hear what she was trying to tell him.

The silence that had fallen when he did not straight away reply stretched endlessly and had her nerve ends ragged, until in the end she just had to look at him.

What she had expected, she had not given herself time to ponder. Most likely he would be looking at her with an expression that said, 'Who the hell's pressing you?' But his expression was telling her nothing of the sort. His good humour had gone, certainly, but the set look to his suddenly deadly serious face made her feel choked up again. And Ellis was then answering her statement, with a tightly controlled question—the way he asked it telling her that this was one time when he wanted a straight answer to a straight question, and that he would settle for nothing less.

'May I know why it is you don't want to see me again?' he asked, a tension about him so that he did not appear to be breathing as he waited for the straight answer she just could not give.

Dumbly she stared at him. It flashed through her mind that it seemed to be of some importance to him that she give him a true answer. And it was just not in her then to lie to him.

'Is it that you're afraid of being tempted should we see each other many more times?' he asked, insisting, she saw, that she did not run away from the question, insisting that she replied.

Fleetingly, she thought of making some sour challenging remark about his conceit. Perhaps an airy comment about him not being able to take what she said without an inquest because he was too conceited to think that any girl wouldn't rush to answer his knock at her door would suffice. But the idea died. No matter how she had tossed that remark about in the past, conceited was something he was not. Besides which, with Ellis refusing to budge, the sheer force of those dark eyes alone, steady on hers, seemed to be tearing away from her that protective cover of the airy type of comment she had found so useful in the past.

As though she was compelled then, her sentence fractured, at last some of the truth was dragged by him from her.

'You—were right—Ellis,' she told him, 'w-when you said what you did about—about once hurting me very much.' Her throat had become dry, there was pain in her, some pain in him too, she felt suddenly. But she had to look away from him when, making herself go on, she revealed her reason for not wanting to see him again. 'I c-can't let you do that to me again,' she choked.

Emotion had been in her as her voice faded to a whisper. But, after agonising moments of wondering, when he had nothing to say, if she had told him too much, when Ellis's voice did hit her ears she heard raw emotion there, as he asked:

'You're saying that the—decision—I took eight years ago has cost me your trust, once and for all?'

Tears inside were threatening to submerge her at the naked note in his voice; the emotion in him was almost beyond her bearing. But because it was the way it had to be, unable to look at him, Sorrel told him, her own voice ragged:

'You said "Be happy", Ellis. All I know is that—I can be happier without you.'

His hand came beneath her chin to force her head up, and before she was anywhere near to trying to disguise her overwhelming sadness, Ellis was making her look at

him. And as his eyes held hers, his hand moved to the
side of her face, his touch, his hold, like a benediction
when for ageless moments he stood like that just
looking into her unhappy eyes.

Had Sorrel not been feeling so disjointed inside, had
she not been conscious of only one thing, that she
would regret it for evermore if she weakened now, she
was not sure that she would not have collapsed against
him when, his voice thick, gravely Ellis told her:

'I do love you, you know.' With shock rippling through
her, all she was capable of then was to stare numbly at
him. But if she had thought she had misheard what he had
said, when he continued, 'I love you, so very much,
Sorrel,' she had confirmation that she had heard him right
the first time. 'I always have,' he ended.

Gently then he kissed her, and tears were falling
inside her like rain. For as he raised his head, his kiss of
farewell broken, Sorrel was breaking up inside—for she
knew then that Ellis had accepted that she did not want
to see him again.

He did not stay to kiss her again. When he knew full
well that he could get a response from her, with her
telling him that she could be happier without him and
refusing to back down from that statement, he had not
attempted to kiss her again. But quietly he left her
apartment.

And Sorrel wept that night as she had not wept in
years. She had not wanted Ellis to hurt her again, but
she *was* hurt. She had told him she did not want to see
him again, but oh, how much did she want to see him
again. Oh God, she wept again into her already sodden
pillow, why did he have to tell her he loved her?

When morning came, she was able to think more
calmly. Though a glance in her bathroom mirror told her

she would be housebound that day, for nothing would reduce the swelling of her tear-puffed eyelids.

Food having no appeal, she made herself a cup of coffee and pondered on what choice had she but to tell him what she had. Ellis might have told her that he loved her, but he had loved Wenda Sykes too once, and never would she forget his unloving look for his ex-fiancée that night at the theatre.

Remembering that contemptuous look, Sorrel knew she just wouldn't be able to take it should she brave telling him where her finances came from and she received that same look from him. He might have said he loved her, but his love for Wenda had soon died, hadn't it?

Aware of her frailty where he was concerned, with part of her pushing at her to go to him, to tell him everything, Sorrel knew that she just could not do it. Ellis had rejected her love once before, she just could not face a second rejection.

By lunchtime, having thought over every word that had passed between them a dozen times, she knew that the part of her that had urged that she go to see him had taken a severe beating. She was then of the opinion that she would have made a fine fool of herself had she done anything of the sort. Tears were again in her eyes when, food still having no appeal, lunchtime saw her busy knocking picture hooks into the wall which Ellis had offered to come early and see to for her.

Perhaps she did use more force than necessary, but anger she was glad of had spurted in her as she slammed the picture hooks in with a rolling pin. For dissecting his statement about loving her, that 'I always have', with which he had ended, she was to see then that it was nothing but a blatant lie.

It looked as though he had always loved her, didn't it, she sniffed, wiping tears away with the back of her hand. Love for Sorrel Maitland hadn't stopped him falling in love with *and* getting engaged to someone else, had it?

When a couple of weeks had passed with no Ellis calling her on the phone or calling at her flat, Sorrel knew she had been right to think that it was all over. Ellis had accepted, as she had thought, that she did not want to see him again—that she would be happier for not seeing him. Oh God, what a lie that was!

At the beginning of the third week since she had sent Ellis out of her life, Sorrel booked a place at a secretarial college, to begin her refresher course at a date in September.

But September seemed an age away, and she needed to keep herself busy. Already her old sophisticated life style seemed to be years away. She had no wish to contact old acquaintances or to resume a way of life which, she had faced, had never been hers anyway.

With the thought in mind that she would spend some time redecorating her flat, that weekend Sorrel journeyed to her parents' home. Her father had always done his own decorating, he would tell her how to go about it.

Her mother was in the front garden when Sorrel drove by the low hedge that fronted the pretty cottage that had been her old home. But Helen Maitland, her head bent to her fine display of roses, did not see or hear her daughter until Sorrel had pushed her way through the wicket gate and was halfway up the path.

'Why didn't you . . .!'

'Let you know I was coming,' Sorrel finished for her, kissing her mother's cheek and then standing back to explain, 'I knew if I did that you'd drop everything and spend hours of this lovely weather baking a welcome in the kitchen.'

Helen Maitland had green fingers and loved her garden, but after a brief study of her daughter, she turned and led the way indoors, her only comment:

'You've lost weight. You could do with some home cooking.'

The rest of that Saturday passed pleasantly, with Sorrel telling her parents about her new flat, and picking her father's brains for tips on paperhanging. But on Sunday when he suggested, and was seconded by her mother, that she take herself off for a walk to get some colour into her cheeks, Sorrel, obeying some inner compulsion, went for a drive instead.

She knew what lay behind that compulsion when she found herself in Kinglingham. Always before she had avoided going anywhere near the area where she and Ellis had worked in such harmony. But that Sunday, Sorrel found the courage to go back.

When she saw that the old brick-built workshop had been pulled down and that a new and larger modern construction had taken its place in the shape of a dry-cleaners, she saw that it was over. There was not so much as a trace of anything there, real or imagined, of what she and Ellis had shared. Sorrel turned her car around and, moist-eyed, hoped with all she had that soon that ache inside would be gone, with no lingering trace to catch her out and wound at the least expected moment.

She left Salford Foley on Sunday evening. 'Stay until the morning,' her mother had tried to detain her. But she shook her head.

'It's been lovely,' she said. 'But first thing tomorrow I want to be in a wallpaper shop.'

Following her father's advice, given that she had one
or two minor mishaps and encountered a snag in that
whoever had built the house where she had her flat had
never heard of straight walls, inside two weeks she had
her small flat decorated throughout, and was looking
around for something else which would keep her fully
occupied until her college course started.

But with nothing presenting itself, the idea of going
to Salford Foley for another weekend was rejected
since, feeling restless, she was sure her restlessness
would show. Her mother was bound to pick it up, and
Sorrel did not want her parent to start to worry about
her. A newspaper was to hand, and she took it up and
scanned idly through the What's On columns.

An exhibition of china dolls did not appeal very
much. Nor did the stamp fair. Her eyes skimmed the
rest of the page, then backtracked to the Art section
where an exhibition of landscapes was announced. That
was one exhibition she very definitely was not going to
visit, she thought.

But five minutes later she was wondering, why
shouldn't she go? Was she such a coward that, just
because Ellis happened to own a few landscapes, she
was afraid she might bump into him?

What did it matter if he was there anyway? she
counter-argued. She could well bump into him
anywhere. Hadn't she decided to be a new person? Was
that new person still going to cling on to the old and
avoid going to any place where she thought Ellis might
be? What was she afraid of anyway?

Becoming irritated with herself and wishing she had
never seen the arts notice, she recalled something she
had read about two old friends who hadn't seen each
other for years but who had, of all places, bumped into

each other on the Great Wall of China, and she saw that the coincidence she was worried about, that of bumping into Ellis if she went to the art gallery, just wouldn't happen. Coincidences, she saw, just didn't happen like that. It was only when one *didn't* expect them to happen that they did. Why, she had to look no further than that coincidence of bumping into Ellis that first weekend she had gone to Rod Drury's home to know that.

And anyway, she thought when later, her confidence needing a boost, she was dressed in one of her smartest outfits and had left her flat, it was more than likely that if Ellis was not at this moment enjoying the peace and solitude of his country home, he was entertaining somewhere a creature not unlike that blonde she had seen him dancing with.

The art gallery was hushed and quiet when she went in, but within minutes Sorrel was thinking, I shouldn't have come. For Ellis was haunting her. In every landscape she saw him. Memory was there of him, of his home, of that Saturday when he had taken her into his home out of the rain.

Oh, Ellis, she cried inwardly. And at that moment she felt so in need of support that she moved to a wide pillar and in a spot where no one could see her, leant up against the pillar until the moment had passed.

When her weakness had gone, Sorrel decided that now the challenge to her courage was satisfied in that she had braved coming to the art gallery—had braved that chance in a million that Ellis might choose that particular gallery in which to spend his Saturday afternoon—she could now honourably go home.

But before she could make any move to step away from the concealing pillar, great clamouring alarm signals were going off in her head. For clearly in the

quietness of her surroundings, suddenly she heard the
voice of someone she guessed was the proprietor,
warmly greeting someone who had just come in.

'Good afternoon, Mr Galbraith,' he said. 'The
painting I telephoned you about . . .'

Frozen, rooted to the spot, she did not hear the rest
of what the proprietor said. Panic-stricken, with no
intention of going anywhere near to the front entrance,
she searched feverishly for another way out.

As she tried desperately for calm, panic took her
again when she heard that it *was* Ellis. 'I'll take a look
now, Charles,' she heard him say. She'd know his voice
anywhere!

Panic rioting through her, she retained enough brain
power to realise that if Ellis was looking at a painting
near the front door, then it had to be by way of a back
door that she made her escape.

Hoping that Ellis had his eyes on the painting he was
there to see, while keeping in a close line with the row
of pillars, on winged feet she went down the length of
the gallery. The thought just did not touch down that
she could just as easily have gone the other way and
have favoured Ellis with an airy wave should he take his
eyes from his inspection of the picture and glance her
way. Panic had hold of her as she saw a door to her left,
and made for it.

Fire regulations alone, she thought, must decree that
there was a second way out, and her hand was on the
door handle. With a speed born of her panic, she swiftly
had the door open, and the next second she had shot
into a room on the walls of which hung framed
paintings.

But she was to notice nothing of the content of the
paintings. For as, winded, a gasp broke from her, with

staring, unbelieving eyes, she saw and recognised the man and woman who were also in the room and were seated on a chaise-longue. So at that moment was Sorrel recognising, too, that her thoughts earlier on coincidences occurring when one was not expecting them had been right.

For a venomous look in the eyes of the tight-mouthed woman who had started to rise told Sorrel that coincidence had played its hand once more. Because never had Cynthia Armitage or her husband ever shown the smallest interest in art—yet in an art gallery was where they both were! And by the look of it, Cynthia, her face starting to contort with fury, was not going to let Sorrel get away this time without hearing all she had been storing up to tell her.

'*You again!*' she shrieked, her strident voice echoing resoundingly in the hushed surroundings.

Another sort of alarm shooting in Sorrel, she sent a panicky look to the door she had left open. But Cynthia Armitage had witnessed her glance, and had wasted no time in going to place herself in between Sorrel and the door.

'Oh no, you don't!' she raged. 'You're not going to walk away this time with your nose in the air. By the time I've finished with you . . .'

'Everybody can hear you,' broke in her husband, trying to shush her.

'You shut up and be quiet!' she shrieked at him. 'I'm talking to Sorrel Maitland, not you, and I don't care who the hell hears me! It's more than about time everybody knew what a cunning, conniving bitch little Miss-butter-wouldn't-melt Sorrel Maitland is!'

'Please,' begged Sorrel, colour draining from her face at hearing her name shouted not once, but twice. If Ellis

was still in the building, he must have heard it. 'Please
d . . .'

'Please,' Cynthia Armitage threw back at her,
nowhere near started yet, 'I'll be damned if I'll do a
thing to . . .'

Two men hurrying into the room made her break off
and move away from the door. Though since she
obviously had no objection to entertaining the whole
street, she would soon have been back on course again,
had not Ellis Galbraith chosen to take charge. With one
look to Sorrel's by now ashen face, he gave her a look
that could have been meant to be reassuring. But it did
nothing to make her feel that she would not rather die
than face the scene she just knew that there was no
escaping from.

'If you'd like to attend to your other clients, Charles,'
he turned to address the man who had so swiftly
followed him in, 'I'll deal with this.' And with another
reassuring look to Sorrel, 'Miss Maitland is a friend of
mine,' he told him.

That Ellis was clearly a valued client was plain to be
seen when the look on Charles' face changed from one
of being torn, to one of relief. He departed quickly,
closing the door behind him in case the yelling broke
out again.

It was a wise precaution. For no sooner had Cynthia
Armitage recovered from this unexpected happening,
than she was off again in full throttle, and ranting at
Ellis.

'Sorrel Maitland is a friend of yours, is she?' Her eyes
had not missed the expensive cut of his suit. 'Well, if
you take my advice, you'll give up her friendship if you
know what's good for you!'

'I can only assume, from that statement, that Miss

Maitland has declined to have your friendship,' said Ellis smoothly, not in the slightest ruffled that Cynthia Armitage was going an ugly shade of purple at his choice of words, as he added, 'From my short acquaintance with you, I can hardly say that I blame her.'

'Why, you . . .!' she bellowed, looking at her husband for support. But, not getting any, she went into a rage as she screamed, 'You won't be so cocky when she's conned you like she conned my father!'

Oh God, Sorrel thought, wanting to run somewhere and hide. Cynthia was going to tell him everything, she knew she was, and there wasn't a thing she could say or do to stop her. She felt too paralysed to move, too paralysed to speak, to beg Ellis not to listen to her, for she knew, even as the look in his eyes went like cold steel, that there was no way he could shut the goaded Cynthia up. Soon that steel in his eyes would change to disgust, not for Cynthia, but for her.

'Your words are slanderous, madam,' she heard him address Cynthia. 'I warn you now to be careful what you say.'

'Careful!' Cynthia snapped, her face working viciously. 'It's not *me* who needs to be careful, it's *you*, if you aren't to be taken in by that cunning, green-eyed, deceitful bitch!'

Sorrel saw a muscle jerk in Ellis's jaw. She saw his hands clench at his sides. And she wanted him to go. But he was not going. He was staying right where he was, his chin tilted aggressively as he told Cynthia Armitage:

'If it's Miss Maitland's beautiful green eyes to which you refer, then I can tell you that never, and I presume to have known her far longer than you, have I ever seen cunning or deceit in them.'

'You wouldn't, would you?' bounced back shrilly. 'She'd keep it well hidden, wouldn't she, while she was trying to con you. You just be careful and follow my advice—never introduce her to your father, or she'd do him for thousands, like she took my father for thousands!'

Sorrel's knees threatening to buckle she saw the expression on Ellis's face change as Cynthia's tirade came to an end. There was an alert look to him as what had been said registered, and Sorrel knew then that it was only a matter of time before that alert look changed to a look of utter contempt.

'Ah, you didn't know that, did you?' Cynthia was going on triumphantly. She had not missed, either, that she had just given him food for thought. 'Didn't it ever dawn on you to wonder where she got her money?' she pounced. And drawing a quick breath, while she thought she still held Ellis's attention, she went storming on, 'Whose money do you think pays for the swanky apartment she lives in? Whose money do you think pays for every expensive rag she has on her back?' And while Sorrel was gripping hard on to the back of the chaise-longue, her worst fears were realised, as, not stopping for breath this time, Cynthia Armitage ranted on, 'My father—that's where her money comes from— my father! That woman,' she told him spitefully, untruthfully, though that hardly mattered now, Sorrel thought, 'has lied and cheated to get every penny she could!'

Sorrel had been ready to faint before Cynthia Armitage, an unmistakable light of victory in her eyes, had come to an end. But the assassination of her character to the man who mattered most in her life had not finished yet, as, ignoring or not seeing the narrow-eyed look Ellis was favouring her with, Cynthia went on to taunt him:

'What do you think of her now? What do you think of a beautiful green-eyed bitch who worms her way into an old man's affections the way she did? An old man, I might add, who was in his dotage and susceptible to women of her sort—what do you think of someone like her who gets a befuddled old man to leave her a packet in his will when he died?'

Her damnation complete, Sorrel was not sure that she was not going to faint. The blackening of her had been vile, but thorough. And now, it seemed, Cynthia had no more to say but was eagerly awaiting for Ellis, won over to her side by all she had told him, to add his own comments for the villainous female she had outlined.

Her mouth arid, Sorrel could not look at him. She did not want to hear what he had to say. Had her legs felt stronger she was not sure that she would not have gone running out of there to avoid hearing his castigation. But if stay she must, then there was no way she was going to look at him and see that mortifying contempt she knew had to be there in his eyes. She had thought she could not take his contempt, but, since she could not run, it would appear that she had no choice.

CHAPTER TEN

IN an agony of torment, Sorrel felt beaten and degraded. But she was never more aware that the way she was feeling then would be as nothing compared to the way she would be feeling when Ellis had finished wiping the floor with her. She did not have to wait long for him to begin.

But, when she had been expecting him to lash her, to destroy her with comments on her avaricious likeness to his ex-fiancée, to her utter astoundment she heard that it was not her whom Ellis was rounding on but— Cynthia Armitage!

Stupefied, Sorrel's eyes shot startled to him when his voice curt, hostile, as she had thought it would be, though not for Cynthia, she heard him say:

'If you have not quite finished your attempt to ruin Miss Maitland's good name, then before you add anything else I think I should warn you that one more outrageous word in the same vein—to me or to anyone else—and I will personally sue you for defaming her.'

'You will *what*!' Sorrel was not the only one to look at Ellis in amazement. 'Didn't you understand what I was telling you!' Cynthia Armitage shrieked. 'That girl there sucked up to my father until he . . .'

'I heard every lie you uttered,' Ellis cut her off, his voice ominously quiet. 'Indeed, against all inclination, I gave you more than a fair chance to reveal some trace of mitigation for the harridan you are, but I saw none. And now I've heard enough.'

'No, you damn well haven't!' screeched Cynthia, throwing her husband a hating glare that the best he could do to back her up was to stand there shuffling his feet. 'My father left her . . .'

'If your father made a bequest to Miss Maitland,' Ellis cut her off sharply, his patience fraying, 'then I have every confidence that he did so because he knew her for the kind and sensitive person she is.'

Gaping, stunned by what was happening, Sorrel realised that Ellis had soon sorted out who the man was whom she had told him she loved dearly; for he was going on:

'I know for a fact that Miss Maitland was very fond of your father. Which is more . . .'

'And his wallet,' broke in Cynthia, her face ugly with rage that things were going very differently from the way she had expected.

But Ellis had had enough. Without wasting time in further argument, he went striding to the door. 'You will oblige me by leaving these premises, and taking that,' he added, pointing to the uncomfortable-looking Leslie, 'with you, before I lose my temper and throw the pair of you out.'

Still clutching hard on to the back of the chaise-longue, Sorrel had time only to register that if Ellis had not yet lost his temper then she didn't want to be around when he did, when she saw Leslie Armitage had taken note of the hard glint in Ellis's eyes that said he had meant exactly what he had said, and had moved to take hold of his wife's arm.

'We were waiting to see the owner of this place,' he mumbled, 'but—but it will do another day.'

Cynthia too had got the message, and did not appear to take very kindly to the idea of being physically

ejected on to the pavement. Though, even while
blanching, she had to try one last stab before she
scuttled off with her husband.

'She . . .' she couldn't resist.

'Do I see you in court?' challenged Ellis, everything
about him saying that he had never gone in for making
idle threats.

'Damn you!' seethed Cynthia, but she knew she was
beaten as she hurried away.

Impatience was still in Ellis's face as he closed the
door with a snap. Sorrel knew it before she heard him
mutter, 'My *God*!'

She guessed when he turned to stare sternly at her
that it was her time to be sorted out. She still did not
know how she was going to be able to take it, but she
was grateful to him that he had not gone to town on
her while the Armitages were present.

'I'm—s-sorry you had to—to be—involved in—in
that,' she apologised. It had nauseated her, and by the
stern look of him, Ellis had not found it very pleasant
either.

'I'm glad I was here,' he replied shortly. 'It isn't in
you to gutter-fight.'

'Because I didn't defend myself, you mean?' she asked,
and knew as she asked it that she had left herself wide
open for him to demand what defence did she have.

But she was to be startled again. For Ellis did not
seem to need to hear her defence! He seemed to know,
without her having to tell him, that it was not in any
way as Cynthia had told it! For all he said was:

'That screeching shrew would never have let you get a
word in anyway.' And, when Sorrel was still expecting
to be trounced, she was to be dumbfounded that as Ellis
looked at her, he had nothing more to say than, 'You're

still pale—will you be all right if I leave? I can drop you off at your flat if you like.'

'I'm—fine,' she managed quietly, her heart starting to drum at the thought that, just like that—no third degree, no questions or recriminations—Ellis would leave or drop her off at her flat, the matter done with, nothing more to be said, and—not a contemptuous look for her in sight! 'I've—g-got my car not far away,' she added, a choky sensation coming to her as some truth pushed at her and tried to get through.

His hand went to the door handle, that same look on his face that had been there that first night in her new flat when he had kissed her farewell and accepted that she did not want to see him again. And as she sensed the truth pushing to get nearer and nearer to the surface, it saw her wanting to stop him before he went through that door and out of her life.

'Why . . .?' she found her husky voice to halt him when, as if in slow motion, that door handle began to turn. Unmoving, Ellis looked at her, his face stern still as he waited to hear what she had started to say. 'Why did you do what you just did?' she asked in a confused rush. 'B-back me, I mean—against Cynthia Armitage— just now.'

His hand fell away from the handle, but he did not move from his position by the door. And his face was unsmiling when, looking steadily at her, he said:

'Over eight years ago, I fell in love with an honest seventeen-year-old, more sensitive than I saw at the time.' Drumming ceased to be the word to describe what Sorrel's heart was doing then. 'At twenty-five,' he went on, his gaze still fully on her, 'that girl may have changed her outer covering, but that honest person she always was is still there.'

His blind belief in her honesty turned Sorrel's legs to jelly. Something inside her seemed to snap then, and she was clutching harder than ever on to the back of the chaise-longue, as the words faltered from her:

'Do you . . .' her voice broke, and she had to swallow hard before she could try again, 'do you still—love—that girl? D-do you still love her now—now that—that you've heard that she's—no better than your ex-fiancée?'

The serious look on his face gave her no indication of what he would answer. And yet his answer was suddenly so very important to her—if it was the answer she wanted.

'Need you ask?' he replied. Which just wasn't enough. She had to have more. If she was to crash through the barrier that had been eight years in the building, this barrier she had made, then she had to have more.

'Was it—your feelings for me that made you go into bat for me without knowing what—if any—defence I had?' she asked haltingly. But she had all the answer she could want in his reply.

'Because I was not in love with Wenda Sykes, I never found it necessary to look beyond the obvious for what she did. With you,' said Ellis, 'my love is such that it doesn't need to hear any defence.'

'You still—trust me—my honesty, after hearing all—all that Cynthia Armitage has said?' she just had to question, unable as she was then to take in the fact that he should love her so much.

'I trust and love you,' stated Ellis, his voice gone harsh, a look coming to him of a man who couldn't take much more. His hand had again gone to the door handle, as, 'Goodbye, Sorrel,' he said tightly, 'I hope you find whatever it is you're looking for in life.'

'Ellis!'

He had his back to her, but she couldn't let him go. He froze as she called his name, but did not turn, but waited as, a ton weight lifting from her, Sorrel saw how blindly he had trusted her, and as courage surged up in her, she saw how completely she could trust him. He had hurt her so bitterly once, but all of a sudden, she just knew that he would never knowingly hurt her again.

'Ellis,' she said again, to keep him there, terrified now that he would go out of her life before she had got it all together. There were still some answers outstanding, but if she was ever to find happiness, she saw then that she had to trust him as blindly as he had trusted her.

'Oh, Ellis,' she said on a shaky breath, 'I think I've just found what I'm looking for.'

His back was still to her, and with tears of hope, feeling the trust in him that she had been searching for suddenly there in her, Sorrel put all her faith in that trust as she said:

'Ellis, you wouldn't—marry me, would you?'

Through her tears she saw shock take him as beneath his suiting his shoulders jerked rigid. What she had just asked was the last thing he had expected to hear, she knew. But when, slowly, he turned and through tears shimmering in her eyes she saw his expression was little short of grim, Sorrel knew that she had to stay in there with her trust, even when, not coming any nearer, he questioned bluntly:

'Why?'

She wished he would smile. Wished that the corner of his mouth would quirk in that haunting way it sometimes did. But there was not a smile about him, nothing there to help her out but the trust she had suddenly found that said he would not reject her a second time. Holding firmly on to that trust, Sorrel blinked back tears.

'A-at seventeen,' she told him, 'I was head over heels in love with you.'

Ellis's face had a strained, taut look, the skin seemed stretched over his cheekbones, his voice gritty, as he questioned, 'And now? What do you feel for me now?'

'And now——' she began, not wanting him standing coldly over by the door. She wanted to be in his arms. Quite desperately did she need to be in his arms as she told him, 'I love you with the whole of my heart.' She saw a pulse begin to beat in his temple, and it was all starting to pour out from her then. 'I knew when I met you again at the Drurys' that I'd never stopped loving you. Even as I tried to tell myself I was cured of you, I . . .' she stopped, and when he made no move to come and take her into his arms, she was faltering again as a sudden thought came. 'If—if you don't want marriage,' she said, remembering how the thought of marriage had appalled him eight years ago, 'then—then that's all right by me.'

'You're saying that you'd be mine without marriage?' he frowned the question.

'If that's what you want,' she replied solemnly, and was in panic again, but only briefly, when he replied:

'I want neither you nor marriage, if all this—your offering yourself to me—stems from nothing more than gratitude for what happened just now with that Armitage bitch.' Her flutter of panic squashed, Sorrel heard that Ellis's voice had gone harsh again, as he asked grimly, 'Is it to do with that?'

As honest as he expected her to be, Sorrel shook her head. 'I was horrified when you came in through that door,' she confessed. 'I knew Cynthia Armitage would just love an audience she could revile me in front of. Your claiming to be my friend made it doubly certain that she'd make as much as she could out of her father leaving me some money. He was a dear man,' she told him, 'but I was terrified that when she had told you her version of the way it was, I would see nothing but loathing and contempt in your eyes for me. But,' Sorrel went on, not a word of interruption coming from Ellis as he insisted on finding out if it was from love or gratitude that she had offered herself to him, 'but— while being grateful, of course, that you didn't range yourself on her side, when blindly you trusted me so much that you didn't believe I could be like she was making out I was, I suddenly knew that I—could trust you. That—that I could tell you about my love for you, because . . .'

'Come here.'

His face stern still, Ellis had cut her off. But his 'Come here' was a command, and Sorrel obeyed it. She had said she trusted him, and it was so. Without hesitation she left the spot where she had taken root, came from the chaise-longue and walked over to the door.

She stopped walking when she was about a foot away from him, her eyes unblinking on his when for long hard seconds dark eyes searched her face. If he truly loved her, she thought, he would take her in his arms.

When one hand did leave his side, her heart fluttered crazily. But Ellis did not take her in his arms. At the sound of footsteps nearing the door his hand took hold of her upper arm.

'We're going to be interrupted,' he said tensely. 'I've waited too long to want anyone barging . . .' he broke off as the door handle turned, and his face was unsmiling as he asked, 'Are you going to come with me?'

Her heart beats erratic, even if Ellis had not answered her proposal, Sorrel was not in a mind to return to the girl who had hidden away behind a false front.

'Anywhere,' she replied, and felt the fingers on her arm tighten, all her trust there in that one word.

Ellis moved at speed then. 'I'll ring you,' he tossed at the man Charles who had entered the room without Sorrel being fully aware of it. And she was through the door and out of the gallery, and seated beside Ellis in his Jaguar, with no thought in her head to wonder where he was taking her, or to remember that her own car was parked not too far away.

When Ellis pulled up in front of an exclusive-looking apartment block and hurried her inside, she knew that it was to his flat he had brought her.

Though not one word did he have to say to her until he had turned his key in the lock of his apartment door and had ushered her through it. With his hand on her arm again, he took her with him into his sitting room. Then he halted her in front of a deep, wide couch.

For long wordless moments Ellis just looked at her. Then, his expression unsmiling still, his hands came up to her hair, his fingers searching to find the pins that secured her chignon.

Without demur, her heart wildly racing, Sorrel stood while he released every last pin. But only when her hair was cascading around her shoulders did he speak.

'Now,' he said, a look of satisfaction relieving his severe expression, 'now you look more like my little Sorrella.'

'You—used to call me that—in the old days,' Sorrel reminded him, her nerves jumping, her voice staccato.

'I've forgotten nothing about you—or the old days,' he replied. But then, to her utter relief, as his voice went throaty, so the words broke from him, 'For God's sake come here!' and Ellis was not waiting for her to move, but had hauled her into his arms, those arms becoming tight bands around her, as he said, 'Have you any idea what sheer unremitting hell these last five weeks have been?'

'If they've been th-the same for you as they've been for me,' Sorrel answered, all hurt and pain washing away from her to be held so securely in his arms, 'then hell doesn't begin to cover it.'

There was no pretence in what she had said. No pretence in the honest love-filled eyes that looked at him when Ellis pulled back to see her face. Time stood still then, as for uncounted moments she just looked at him while he devoured her every feature. She as content just to stand quietly within the circle of his arms, as Ellis seemed to need, and be content, just to hold her.

Unmoving, she stood when after a while, as if he could not believe that she was there with him, he raised a hand to touch her cheek, to stroke that hand gently down the side of her face.

A groan broke from him then, and he just had to kiss her. It was a kiss that lengthened. A kiss, as Sorrel held back nothing and entwined her arms around him, that was to leave her breathless.

As she sank with him down on to the couch, joy broke in her to hear the fractured, 'My—love,' that left him. Then Ellis was claiming her lips again like a man starved for that possession. More uncounted minutes passed, for Sorrel had been starved too and was as hungry for his touch as he was hungry to have her unrestrained response.

With his body close to hers on the couch, she felt one of his hands in her hair, that hand caressing down her face, to her throat, at her breast. 'Oh, Ellis!' she sighed, and had both his arms around her as he pressed her to him and kissed her mouth, his mouth then trailing kisses over the flush of ever-increasing passion on her face.

Her hand, straying up to touch his face, had him taking hold of that hand, his eyes holding a warm light as they looked into hers. It was then that she saw the quirk she loved so much come to the corner of his mouth when, his voice husky in his throat, he said softly:

'If you intend to carry on in this way, Miss Maitland, then I really think I shall have to do something about your proposal—without delay.'

Glorying that, as if those eight years had never been, Ellis could so easily tease a smile from her, all at once Sorrel realised that although he had been showing signs of thoroughly welcoming the way she had reacted to his kisses, that fully responding had not been the only area in which she had been not a little forward.

A little more colour had pinkened her face when, taking a gulping breath, she just had to ask, 'Do you—want to marry me, Ellis?' And as anxiety started to rush in, without giving him time to answer, she was saying quickly, 'You don't have to if . . .' His mouth coming down over hers effectively cut off the rest of her sentence.

But Sorrel had her answer when, after moments of being able to do nothing but respond fully to him again, his voice gruff from the soaring passion they shared, suddenly Ellis had pulled her to sit up. And having let some daylight between their two bodies, he said:

'My need to hold you, to make love to you, will have to wait. I've put you through too much hell in the past to take you now with doubts still in your mind.'

'I don't . . .' She would have told him of her new-found trust in him then, that her doubts were not doubts about her trust in him. But Ellis silenced her, though he could not deny his need to hold her as, with an arm about her shoulders, he sat half turned so he could look at her, and said:

'Of course I want to marry you, woman. I've always wanted to marry you.' Going on to make her eyes go wide as he revealed, 'It was always my intention to marry you, way back when you were a teenager.' His eyes went bleak, but only for a moment as he told her, 'You have no idea of my agony in thinking I'd left it too late.'

Her wide eyes fixed on his, Sorrel recalled how he had said that he had always loved her. And with that renewed trust in her for him, there was peace in her heart at last. For her trust in him was complete that even if she could not understand how that could be— that he had always loved her—if he had said it was so, then she believed him.

But that he loved her, was there in the way he looked at her, she saw. There in the way, when it looked a moment ago as though he would make love to her until she was fully his, he had drawn back for her sake, for the sake of the doubts he thought she still nursed.

Even though he had so cruelly dismissed her, yet was maintaining now that he had meant to marry her even then, Sorrel trusted his word. Trusted his love. So that with that trust in her strong, it was more from remembering how he had heard every word of Rod proposing marriage to her, than from questioning his statement that he thought he had left it too late, that she smiled into his eyes and said:

'You thought, that night when you blatently eavesdropped when Rod Drury asked me to marry him, that I was going to say "yes"?'

'Don't remind me,' said Ellis. 'I came the nearest I ever came to going into heart failure that night.' His fingers seemed unable to resist stroking down her cheek as, 'How I managed to stay put I shall never know,' he owned. 'There were moments of silence when I was sure he was kissing you. Black jealous murder was in my heart then, so that it was all I could do not to come and tell him for you that if you were going to marry anyone, it was going to be nobody but me.'

'Oh, Ellis!' she sighed, loving every word he was telling her. 'That almost makes up for the jealousy that made me want to scratch the eyes out of that blonde you danced too many times with at the Drurys' wedding anniversary party.'

'It worked, then,' he said, his grin flushing out her grin, as with happiness bubbling over, she accused:

'You devil—you tried to make me jealous on purpose?'

'I was ready by then to try anything,' he admitted. 'I'd been as mad as hell with you, but when I'd cooled down I was certain that—despite what you said—on that night I almost made you mine there'd been nothing pre-thought-out in your response. But I knew, by the time I'd analysed everything, that the next time I saw you the barrier you were insisting on raising would have grown higher.'

'Oh, darling,' Sorrel cried softly, 'have I given you such a very hard time?'

'Don't, my love,' he answered swiftly. 'When I think

of the dreadful suffering I've caused you ...' He broke off, and seemed then unable to go on, for he cradled her to him, his hold tender, and for long moments nothing more was said.

But after a while he recovered from the anguish of his thoughts, and tenderly kissed her before, having to pause to clear his throat, he went on.

'To get back to that night. I never intended to go to the Drurys party.'

'You didn't?'

He shook his head. 'After hearing you reject Drury, I was sure you wouldn't be going either. And after the way we'd parted, I was telling myself that even if you were going, I was sure I wasn't interested.'

'You'd got the hump?'

'Cheeky witch—you'd given it to me!'

'I'm dreadful—aren't I?' asked Sorrel, loving him with all her being.

'Quite, quite dreadful,' he agreed, kissing her again purely because he could not resist the temptation of her lips.

'But you came to that party just the same?'

'You'd got me roped and tied,' he owned openly, to her delight. 'I had no intention of going, as I said, but as that evening wore on and I found myself pacing the floor of my home, I discovered I was looking for ways of assaulting that barrier you had erected, so that I might yet get through to the real you.' His eyes were gentle on her as he said, 'My thoughts were turning to how you'd turned out to be so vastly different from the way I'd always imagined you.'

'It was only on the surface,' Sorrel thought she had better mention. His smiling look told her she had no need, that he had seen through her, as he went on:

'To my mind, then; with you acting in an exact opposite way from all my expectations—the hour getting later and later if I was going to put in an appearance—it seemed to me that far from you not being at that party, if you were running true to your new form, then regardless of Drury having proposed and been turned down, you were, at that moment, right there within a few minutes of a fast car drive away.'

'I only went because Rod said his parents' happiness might be dimmed a little if they suspected he was low because . . .' Sorrel broke off, her eyes smiling as she asked, 'You came to that party because you thought I might be there?'

He nodded. 'And wished I'd stayed at home,' he owned, 'when for my pains you told me how dearly you loved the man who was paying your rent.'

'Oh,' said Sorrel, 'I still haven't told you about Mr Ollerenshaw.'

'You don't have to,' he said promptly. 'If the old gentleman provided for you in his will, then I don't need you to tell me that he did so because you were just you with him, with no thought in you of any possible gain there might be at the end of it.'

Tears brimmed in her eyes at his trust in her. 'Oh, Ellis,' she said huskily. 'Mr Ollerenshaw left his daughter well provided for, I promise you. Only . . .' his look said he did not want to hear any more, but when he saw that it seemed important to Sorrel to tell him everything, he let her continue, 'Cynthia has no idea how to handle money, so although he left her and her children most of his fortune, he tied it up so that she can't get it all at once.'

'But your nest-egg you could have right away?' Ellis suggested, seeing without her having to tell him why it was that she was like a red rag to a bull where Cynthia Armitage was concerned.

'Mr Ollerenshaw knew that if he didn't tie it up so that Cynthia received so much every quarter, within a few years, there would be nothing left. The poor dear man,' Sorrel went on quietly, 'he worked so hard to amass his fortune, and had so little rest in his ailing years. But had it not been for him leaving a note in his will saying that if I didn't accept his gift he wouldn't rest easy in his grave then . . .'

'When the Armitage woman kicked up rough, you would have given it up,' said Ellis, seeming to know her as well as she knew herself.

She nodded, 'Not that it would have done Cynthia or the children any good. There was also a proviso that if I didn't accept, then the money was to be used to research the mating habits of the common fieldmouse.'

'They seem to be coping quite well without his money,' commented Ellis. And having observed her while she had been telling him what she had, he said quietly, 'It's obvious to me that you were fond of him— more fond, I should say, than that apology he had for a daughter.'

'She never showed him any affection that I saw,' agreed Sorrel quietly, 'and I lived with them for . . .'

'You *lived* with them? In the same house as that woman?' questioned Ellis, as though the very idea appalled him.

'It wasn't so bad,' Sorrel understated. 'At least— well—oh, how can I lie to you, darling?' she sighed. 'It was foul most of the time, but . . .'

'Why the hell did you stay there?' he interrupted, angry, but only for her, Sorrel knew. 'Were you employed as live-in social secretary of something? Were you . . .' Suddenly he stopped, and reading his look, Sorrel said:

'There's so much we don't know about each other, isn't there?'

His hand caressed her face again. 'So much, my darling,' he agreed. 'Though for my part, there's not much of interest in those void years without you.' He looked lovingly at her then, and asked, 'You trust me, my love?'

'Completely,' she replied unhesitatingly, and was promptly on the receiving end of his kiss.

'My beloved Sorrel,' he breathed, checking the rising passion in him to tenderly kiss her cheek. We've so much wasted time to make up, yet I'm filled with such a longing to touch you all the time, in case this is just some marvellous dream the gods will snatch away from me, that I'm having difficulty in keeping my hands off you.'

'I shan't have the smallest objection to raise if you want to keep your arm around me,' Sorrel replied solemnly.

'You're being forward again,' teased Ellis in return, 'and I love it.'

Then all teasing went from him, as he kissed her again, his hands caressing her breasts, passion mounting once more, so that when he broke his kiss and looked deeply into her eyes, Sorrel was all at sea with the emotion of wanting him.

'When you—touch me—like that,' she said chokily, 'I don't think—I want to talk at all.'

The same need in him was unmistakable from the fire in his eyes. But he did not kiss her again, but told her, 'Never stop wanting me, as all these years I've wanted you, my Sorrella.'

No question of lack of trust on either side then, Sorrel guessing he was trying to cool the temperature a little, rested her head against his shoulder.

'Would you have gone on wanting me, but doing nothing about it, had we not bumped into each other accidentally that night at the Drurys'?' she asked.

'Probably,' he replied, which had her raising her puzzled head to look at him. For the Ellis she knew had always been a man who went after what he wanted. 'But,' he added, 'in answer to the question I can see burning in your eyes—I was of the opinion that I'd already lost you for ever. I thought,' he ended, to make her eyes go shooting wide, 'that you were happily married to someone else.'

'You thought . . .' she gasped, staring at him.

'I was certain of it,' he nodded. 'So certain that when this beautiful cool creature walked into the Drurys' drawing room on the night I'd gone to discuss some business, I was shattered. When Neville Drury and I went to his study, my mind was never less on business. All I could think was that my little Sorrel had come a long way from the beautiful teenager I'd fallen in love with. I couldn't get over the fact that you seemed to be going steady with Rod Drury. But most of all, the one thought that kept returning was, why the hell weren't you wearing a wedding ring.'

'But what made you think I was married!' Sorrel exclaimed.

'You never contemplated marrying anyone?' he asked.

Vigorously she shook her head. 'Never,' she said. 'After you sacked me—when I recovered . . .' she broke off as she saw Ellis frown as though he did not like to remember what his getting rid of her had done to her. Quickly she went on, 'I went to work in the next village for Cynthia Armitage. She wanted a nanny for . . .'

'Nanny? You went to work as a nanny?' Ellis exclaimed. Then as a kind of groan escaped him, his arm firmed about her shoulders, as he said tortuously, 'Oh God—all this time . . .' which meant little to her. Though it became clearer as he went on, 'I thought, right up until the time you told me you'd never had a child, that those two children I saw you with were yours.'

'Mine?' it was her turn to exclaim. And as she remembered, 'But you only thought it was me you saw with the children that day you had business in Kinglingham!'

'With or without those pale streaks of natural gold in your hair, my love,' he said softly, 'I should know you anywhere.' But he was to make her eyes go huge, her face astonished, when he went on to reveal, 'It was not in Kinglingham that I saw you, but in Salford Foley.'

'You were—actually *in* Salford Foley!'

Ellis nodded, his mouth quirking as he said, 'And not on business.'

'You came to—see me?' Staggered, she brought out what her intelligence told her.

Again he nodded, though that suggestion of a smile had gone from him, and his face was serious as he told her, 'I hadn't quite made my mark in the business world then, but I was on my way up—I just couldn't wait to come for you any longer.'

'You . . .' her voice got lost in shock, but she recovered sufficient vocal power to squeak, 'you came—for me!'

'I was hoping with everything in me that I hadn't left it too late,' he confirmed.

'Oh, Ellis,' Sorrel cried. 'Why didn't you come and speak to me!'

'I couldn't,' he replied. 'I'd driven to Salford Foley with half of me knowing I was a fool to pin my hopes on the memory I'd carried with me for five years of you fervently vowing that you would always love me. The moment I saw you on the front lawn of your parents' home, one child tugging at your skirts, a baby in your arms being handled so expertly you just had to be its mother, I was convinced my attitude had killed all the love you had for me stone dead, and that you'd soon afterwards married, and had those babies you'd scared the hell out of me by mentioning that last but one time we met.'

Winded by what he had told her, all Sorrel was capable of was to stare at him, stunned, for long, long moments. She recalled how often Cynthia Armitage had told her to 'take those brats from under my feet'. How many were the times, if the weather was fine and sometimes when it wasn't, she had walked pushing both children to her parents' home in the next village. The incident of Arabella pulling on her skirt on the front lawn of her parents' home, she could not remember, but that Ellis had been that close, and she had not known, was staggering. That he had come there specially to collect her rocked her.

'But—but,' she was trying to surface. And, 'Oh, Ellis,' she cried again, 'if only you'd just said "Hello" you would soon have discovered . . .'

'I was in a hell of a state,' he confessed. 'I didn't want to believe what my eyes were telling me—that you were happily married, and had popped in to visit your mother with your children for an afternoon cup of tea. When I heard the little girl try to get your attention by calling you "Mummy", I just had to believe it. My foot went down on the accelerator—I don't remember that drive back to London.'

Sorrel was quiet for a moment or two, then, 'Oh,' she groaned, that same tortured note there that Ellis had used, as she remembered, and told him as she recalled it, 'Arabella was always a perverse child. Her phase of calling me "Mummy", despite all correction, went on for an age.' Another despairing sound for what might have been left her, as she added, 'It only stopped when Cynthia refused to let her out of her room until she got it right, on the day Arabella took to calling her "Nanny".'

'Perishing child,' said Ellis, but without heat, as with another loving look at Sorrel, he leaned over to kiss and to hold her.

Flushed and never more happy, Sorrel pulled back a breathless few minutes later, to ask, the passion of her feelings at that moment threatening to come between her and what she wanted to know:

'Are you saying that you always intended to marry me, even while you were—throwing me out of your flat that day?'

'God, don't remind me,' he groaned. 'I knew before that first time we kissed that I loved you.'

'You did!' she asked, her eyes going wide again in her surprise, remembering the excitement that day he had first kissed her.

'But what I also knew,' he said, taking out a moment to give her surprised mouth a featherlight kiss, before pulling back and going firmly on as though he thought he owed her an explanation for all the heartbreak she had been through, 'was that I had to cool it.'

'Because you didn't want to marry me?' she asked.

'I desperately wanted to marry you,' Ellis contradicted, 'but I was being ridden by ambition. A wife, children, would have to come first with me—I couldn't take the risk of our marriage turning sour, of our love turning to hate—of our marriage ending in divorce.'

Suddenly Sorrel was seeing how on the right track she had been in her thoughts during that long sleepless night after Ellis had ordered her out of his flat eight years ago.

'You mean the way your parents' love ended?' she questioned, and felt his arm tighten about her shoulders.

'You've remembered what I told you about my father having that same fire of ambition and how he never gave a thought when he fell in love that marriage, starting a family, meant there would never be any money to get his plans off the ground?'

Sorrel nodded. 'Is that why you got—rid—of me, because . . .'

'I grew up watching the love my parents had change into hatred,' he told her, the love in his eyes for her healing the memory of that rejection the word 'rid' had brought. 'Life in that house became one constant row— I couldn't let that happen to us. Yet what was I to do? You were seventeen, and I was in hock up to my ears at the bank and needing for years to plough everything I earned back into the business. You wanted commitment *then*, and I loved you too much to marry you and to risk our love turning into hatred—to risk waking up one morning and finding that, now you were married to me, the laughter that had always been in your eyes was suddenly no longer there.'

There was no thought of reproach in her when he had finished speaking, only a feeling that she would have been better able to bear that rejection had she known, as the words slipped from her:

'Oh, Ellis, how I wish you'd told me all this at the time!'

'It wouldn't have done any good to tell you any of it, sweetheart,' he said quietly. 'We'd already gone too far.' Tenderly then, he kissed her brow. Then he was saying, 'While I was able to part from you with just a few chaste kisses, I thought I could handle it until such time as I was in a position to marry you. But, once we'd gone past that stage of chaste kisses . . .'

'That day I came to your flat because I'd left my keys at home,' Sorrel remembered.

'Exactly,' he said. 'There you were, already talking of babies, of marriage, of us living together. I had to stop you. Had to get you out of my flat, and fast, because having started to make love to you, I wanted you so desperately then, that I knew if I couldn't get you out, within minutes I would be weakening, and taking you.'

'I thought you'd stopped wanting me!'

His mouth quirked, his look gentle, he shook his head. 'How little you knew, my innocent,' he said softly. 'The anguish you caused me, young woman!'

'I—never—knew,' she whispered, and saw Ellis's face fall into solemn lines as he went on to explain.

'While you remained unawakened, I was able to hold my physical need for you in check. But that day, after you'd gone, I was in a cold sweat realising now you'd shown that you wanted me as much as I wanted you—I was still remembering the teenager who had been all woman in my arms—I just had to know that there was now no going back to chaste kisses. That for both our sakes, I had to be tough.'

'So you sacked me,' said Sorrel, knowing that, whatever it had cost them both, he had been right to do what he had. For, try as they might, she saw that once having tasted the delights of fired passion, there would be little chance of any further kisses, remaining chaste. Ellis, more worldly than she, had been able to see that.

His hand came to caress down the side of her face, such a tenderness in his eyes for her as she had never expected to see, 'I had to let you think I didn't care,' he murmured.

'Is that why you straight away started dating Jenny Pearson?'

'Was she the girl who lived in your village?' he asked, obviously having forgotten her name, but the answer to her question there in that he had chosen to date a girl who came from a few streets away.

'You got engaged to Wenda Sykes,' she suddenly remembered.

'Without love,' Ellis reassured her again. 'It happened a year after I'd been forced to face the fact that I'd lost you for ever. It caused no pain when I discovered how she managed to afford a different model outfit each time I saw her.'

'You don't think . . .'

'If you're going to refer to the money that pays for your clothes, don't,' he told her, his face momentarily stern. 'I'll admit I hated not knowing who was paying your rent,' he said, his stern expression leaving, 'but once I knew that—forgive me, darling—that it was not for favours granted, I was hoping with all I had that from somewhere you would find a little of that trust I once crucified, to tell me all there was to know.'

'You wanted my trust?'

'Desperately,' he replied. 'I tried all I could to beat down that high fence you'd erected, tried hard to gain your confidence, to get you to unlock that door of trust—but you weren't having any. I was ready to beg for your trust,' he admitted unashamedly.

'Oh, darling,' Sorrel cried, 'you wanted my trust that badly?'

'I hoped that if I could once again get you to trust me, there might be a chance of getting you to care for me again,' he confessed, taking her hand up to his mouth to tenderly kiss the back of it. 'That's why,' he went on after a moment, 'when I could easily have discovered the answers to the mysteries that surrounded you by going to Salford Foley and asking your parents about you, about the children I'd seen you with, and this sophisticated woman you were trying to be, I stopped myself. I wanted you to tell me—it was important to me that you did.'

'So that—if I told you myself—you would know that I trusted you,' whispered Sorrel, seeing in her mind's eye how casually he would have approached her parents, seeing too, how just like other parents, they wouldn't be able to resist showing off a little about their offspring, and how inside a very few minutes, Ellis would have got from them all that he wanted to know.

Ellis smiled his confirmation. 'I thought my heart would stop when I heard you ask me to marry you,' he confessed. 'For a couple of seconds I couldn't believe it. My God, I thought, she does trust me—she trusts me— she must do. Then—Oh God, is she saying she loves me?'

'All that went through your mind when . . .'

'Yes, my darling,' he said, gathering her up close. 'But it was too much to take in in just a few seconds.'

'So you had to ask why.'

'Thank God you trusted me enough to tell me. These last weeks since you told me plainly that you would be happier never to see me again—and I had to take it—have been hell.' His cheek was near to hers, she kissed it, and was pulled closer still.

With both of them hungry for physical contact, many minutes passed in the flat without a word being spoken. And Sorrel's cheeks had a warm look to them when, still wanting, Ellis pulled his head back to look into her love-filled eyes.

'Thank God,' he said then on a relieved breath, 'even if there are a few gaps in the eight years we have to fill in, that at last we have the most essential matter settled.'

In Sorrel's view, she had been more than a little forward already. 'You mean—er—about us getting married?' she asked uncertainly. But she knew she had got it right, when Ellis kissed the tip of her nose, that quirk breaking as he teased:

'Don't, for the Lord's, sake go coy on me at this stage, Miss Maitland—or I'll make you wait a week before I take you up on your proposal, instead of the three days I have in mind to make you Mrs Galbraith.'

'You wouldn't?' A smile of pure happiness beamed from her as she asked the unnecessary question.

'No,' he agreed, 'I wouldn't. I've waited too damn long as it is,' he growled.

His eyes were on the laughter in her eyes when she heard the words she had doubted hearing that day he had taken her in out of the rain. Though, if what he said broke from Ellis again as if without his known volition, there was no doubt in her mind about what she was hearing this time. For it was all there, in his look, in his fractured breath, as:

'God, how I love you,' he said.